Indecent Danger

Travis Anderson is the picture of success. Handsome, sexy, and rich he could have pretty much any woman he wanted. Sadly, the only ones he seems to find think that size matters. The size of his wallet, that is. He wants a woman to love him for himself. Aubrey Grayson just might be the change he's needed in his life.

Aubrey thinks Travis is an amazing man, with or without his fortune. Growing up in foster care, she learned to appreciate the simple things in life. She's happy going on a picnic and watching the sunset. No wallet needed.

So when Travis takes her on an elegant weekend getaway in Florida, she doesn't care about the beautiful gowns and dripping diamonds. What she does care about is bumping into the hateful man from her past who decides it would be fun to tell Travis all her shameful secrets.

When that man turns up dead, Aubrey quickly becomes a suspect and has to come clean to Travis about everything. Nothing in the world could be worse than admitting the whole sordid story… unless it's being branded a killer.

But there's no way Travis is going to allow Aubrey to go to prison for a murder she didn't commit. If he has to catch the real killer himself, that's just what he'll do.

Indecent Danger

Danger Incorporated

Book Three

BY

OLIVIA JAYMES

www.OliviaJaymes.com

INDECENT DANGER
Print Edition
Copyright © 2015 by Olivia Jaymes

Chapter One

AUBREY GRAYSON'S HIGH heels clicked on the polished marble floors of the luxury suite where she and Travis Anderson would be staying for the next few days. She'd been in some fancy hotels since working for Travis but nothing had prepared her for this. It was far beyond anything she'd ever seen except perhaps on television.

She looked down at the royal blue wraparound dress she wore with a pair of silver sandals, and was glad she'd followed her instincts and dressed up a bit for the journey. Her usual blue jeans and white blouse would have looked out of place in these opulent surroundings.

"Will there be anything else, Mr. Anderson?" the bellman asked after unloading the bags in the two bedrooms. "Shall I send someone up to unpack for you?"

"We're fine, thank you." Travis tipped the man and received a giant smile in return as the bellman retreated out of the door, leaving them alone in the sumptuous suite.

Aubrey had been Travis's administrative assistant for six months and his girlfriend for one so she ought to be used to the wealthy circles in which he traveled, but it still never ceased to amaze her how the one percent lived. It was as far from her own humble background as the moon from the earth.

Placing her purse down on the sofa, she ran her hand over the butter-soft leather while admiring the striped silk throw pillows. The suite was spectacularly over the top.

It was the only way Aubrey could describe it. Large floor to ceiling windows lined one wall that overlooked the emerald green waters of the Gulf of Mexico. But if you didn't want to look at the view, the large living room boasted two pristine beige couches that faced a flat-screen television. The other side of the suite held the wet bar and the dining area, the table large enough to seat six.

Directly in front of her was a round, dark oak coffee table with a crystal vase placed in the center filled with two dozen pink long-stemmed roses.

Her favorite flower and Travis knew it.

She leaned over and breathed in the heady fragrance of a bloom while her fingers caressed a velvety petal.

"They're beautiful. You spoil me."

Travis stepped in behind her and pulled her back against his warm body, nuzzling her neck. "Not nearly as beautiful as you are but I'm glad you like them. You deserve to be spoiled, Bree, and I'm just the man to do it. There is also supposed to be a bucket of champagne around here somewhere so we can celebrate the start to our weekend. Just the two of us."

She nodded toward the bar but didn't move from his embrace, letting herself luxuriate in his hard muscled arms for a little longer than she should. She breathed in his scent feeling slightly light-headed, he smelled delicious with just a hint of spice and citrus to tease her nostrils.

"Just the two of us?" she queried, twisting so she was looking up at his handsome face. "I thought we were here for your friend's annual birthday party. It sounds like the two of us plus about a hundred of his closest friends."

Travis chuckled and quickly pressed a kiss to her forehead before striding over to the bar area. "More like fifty, but you're right—it's still a crowd. Don't worry, there will be plenty of time for just the two of us. I'll make sure of it. Here's that champagne."

When they were alone everything was fine. Aubrey felt comfortable when it was the two of them hanging around his house cooking dinner and watching television. It was when they were with other people that she felt...out of place. It was as if his friends and acquaintances could look right through her and see that she didn't belong there.

She was a foster kid from the streets of Chicago and Travis was a wealthy and well-educated, sought after bachelor. He traveled the world and moved in these circles on a daily basis. All of this was old hat to him while she was simply trying not to stand out like the proverbial sore thumb. She'd hate to embarrass him or herself, but better the latter than the former she supposed.

She still wasn't sure what Travis saw in her. With his short dark hair, vivid green eyes, and all-American good looks, he was adored by women young and old. It was only a matter of time before he moved on to a more suitable female. Someone who dressed in designer fashions and knew which fork to use.

Smiling and showing off that dimple in his cheek, Travis

handed her a champagne flute filled with bubbly golden liquid before lifting his own in toast. His gaze roamed her figure head to toe and it was clear from the warmth in his eyes he liked what he was seeing, which only caused her to grip the crystal flute that much tighter.

"Here's to a wonderful weekend and some quiet time for the two of us."

"Quiet time," she echoed softly, giving him a smile when what she really wanted to do was run back outside and take the first plane back to Montana. She was tempting fate with this weekend away with him and chances were high that it was all going to implode on her at the worst possible moment.

They clinked glasses and she sipped at the cool elixir even as her throat tightened at his words. She had a feeling that "quiet time" was a polite euphemism for something much more intimate and more passionate. The suite might have two bedrooms but Travis had a gleam in his eye that spoke louder than words.

He wanted to make love.

Have sex.

Whatever it was called, Travis was a man of strong appetites and used to getting them fed on a regular basis by a bevy of gorgeous, willing women. When he'd asked Aubrey out she was positive he'd had no idea that he would be kept in a holding pattern for a solid five weeks. She doubted if he'd waited that long since his high school or college days.

Just the thought of her own high school years made her inwardly wince and she deliberately pushed all those disturbing images away. determined to enjoy this time with the man she adored. She changed the subject to get her mind back under control.

"So tell me about this friend of yours that I'm going to meet this weekend."

Aubrey settled onto one of the couches and Travis sat beside her, his hard thigh brushing against hers, a delicious distraction. It hadn't been easy keeping him at arms' length since they'd started dating. He was handsome, smart, funny, and sexy and she was only human. Her dreams were filled with all the naughty things they might do together but hadn't. Yet.

"Our host is Martin Guinness, the hedge fund manager. He was a mentor for me since my Harvard years and he's just an all-around great guy. He basically taught me pretty much everything I know about the business world. He's a financial genius."

"You flatter me, Travis. I'm simply a man who is good at math."

Travis jumped from the couch, a wide grin spreading across his face. Aubrey turned to see a tanned, silver-haired gentleman standing in the still open doorway of their suite. Smiling, he strode forward to shake Travis's hand before they both embraced like long lost friends.

Martin looked younger than the seventy-three years she knew him to be. Maybe it was the relaxed air he had about him that immediately put Aubrey at ease. Normally she felt uncomfortable around Travis's wealthier friends but clearly this man didn't stand on ceremony, eschewing formalities. He reached for her hand and gave her a friendly grin as she also stood to greet their guest.

"You must be Aubrey. I've heard so much about you. I'm

glad you could join us this weekend for a little celebration."

He had a kind twinkle in his eyes that made her smile in return. "Thank you. I hear a happy birthday is in order."

"Thank you. This is really the best gift I could get. All my friends and family gathered in one place. When you get to be my age, my dear, it isn't things that make you happy. It's experiences."

Aubrey couldn't help but agree with those sentiments even though she was much younger than Martin.

"Actually I was hoping I could have a word or two with you, Travis. If you have a few minutes." Martin's smile had disappeared and in its place he wore a frown. "I hate to bother you but it's important. It's regarding what we talked about last week."

Travis nodded, his own expression bland. Aubrey had come to recognize it whenever he talked business that was particularly unpleasant. "Of course. Why don't I meet you down in the bar in about five minutes?"

Martin quickly agreed and exited the suite, leaving Aubrey alone with Travis again. Now there was a definite tension in Travis's shoulders that hadn't been there before Martin arrived, and for a moment she thought about asking him what the meeting was about. She was Travis's assistant so she was often privy to information of a sensitive and confidential nature. However, she didn't get the chance as he abruptly turned on his heel to place his now empty champagne flute on the bar.

"I shouldn't be downstairs too long." He straightened his tie before checking his phone, a frown furrowing his forehead. "Will you be okay up here by yourself?"

Aubrey often wondered what kind of women Travis had dated in the past. He looked worried that she wouldn't be able to entertain herself as if she expected him to be her personal court jester for the weekend.

"I'll be fine. I'll slip into the shower and then relax with a good book until it's time to get ready for the party."

He ran his hands up and down her bare arms, sending a shiver of pleasure up her spine.

"I just want this mini-vacation to be perfect for you, honey."

Everything with Travis was perfect.

It was starting to wear on her nerves.

"It couldn't be any more wonderful," she assured him, standing on her tiptoes to press a kiss to his stubbly cheek. "Go have a drink with Martin. I think I can take care of myself for a little while. It sounded important. Is everything okay with him?"

Travis frowned for only a moment but then gave her a distracted smile. His head was already downstairs with his friend. "It's just business as usual, I'm sure. I'll try and be back in about an hour."

"Take your time. I might even take a nap."

Anything to escape so she could be by herself and think this through. She was beginning to believe she'd made a severe error in judgment coming here this weekend with Travis. Setting her glass on the coffee table, she turned to escape but Travis's hand caught her arm before she could flee into the bathroom.

Travis rubbed his thumb across her palm, setting off a veritable cavalcade of sensations. "Are you okay, honey? You've been really quiet since we got to the hotel."

Of course she was quiet.

She was so damn confused she could barely get out a coherent sentence. If he had any idea all the thoughts that were whirling in her brain he'd be shocked. One minute she wanted to grab his hand, throw him on the bed and make love to him. The next she wanted to chuck her high heels and run out of this fancy resort and away from him.

Frankly, she was a mess.

"I'm fine. Just tired. I'm sure the shower will help revive me though."

"I'll try and be extra quiet when I come back in case you're asleep. Thank you for being so understanding."

Aubrey stood in the middle of the room after Travis left the suite, taking a deep breath to calm her racing heart. She wasn't sure she could keep up the facade of impeccable girlfriend much longer. If he knew who she really was what would he do? She was terrified to find out.

It was only a matter of time before he saw the real Aubrey.

Chapter Two

TRAVIS WAITED UNTIL the busty cocktail waitress had placed two highball glasses filled with eighteen year old Jameson on the table and drifted on to the next patrons before speaking. The bar was dark although it was midafternoon on a sunny day in Florida and thankfully it was almost deserted. It was the ideal spot for a private conversation.

"How can I help you, Martin?"

Travis kept his tone on the neutral side although he could tell his friend and mentor was disturbed by someone or something. They'd had a brief conversation a few weeks ago about Martin investigating some business dealings that his grandson-in-law Bruce Livingston was involved in. Bruce was married to Martin's granddaughter Caroline much to the old man's chagrin. He'd never been in favor of the marriage and Travis couldn't help but agree. Bruce tended to be too self-absorbed and rather shiftless which didn't make him the best husband in the world. Unfortunately Caroline had fallen for Bruce's charm despite his shortcomings.

The older man sighed and swirled the amber liquid in the glass before taking a large gulp. "It's Bruce. I told you I was looking into some of his accounts but I needed to be sure before I said anything."

Martin looked about ten years older than the last time Travis had seen him. Deep grooves around his mouth and eyes, gave the appearance of a deeply tired man. The complete opposite of the fireball of energy everyone was used to.

"And you're sure now?"

"It's insider trading."

The older man's hushed tones didn't detract from the impact of those two words.

Insider trading.

"You're sure?"

Martin nodded, his lips a grim line. "Yes, unfortunately. He's got a girlfriend who has suddenly come into a great deal of money. I checked her out and she's got several brokerage accounts all with different firms. She's made most of her money on stock buys and sells on companies that Bruce is supposed to be researching. Seems like a strange coincidence."

This was the kind of stuff that gave business a bad name. It tarred everyone with the same brush.

"A girlfriend? That seems rather foolhardy to use someone that he can be linked to," Travis observed, still wondering how he could be any help. Martin was the financial genius of the two of them.

"Bruce thinks he's smarter than everyone else. He thinks I don't know that he's dating Iris. Hell, everyone knows, even Caroline. Why she puts up with it I have no idea. I guess she still loves him even though he's a horse's ass."

Caroline was a sweet girl who deserved something better.

She'd married Bruce right out of college in a huge wedding in Hawaii. It should have been a fairy tale but the reality was anything but.

"So how can I help? Do you want to send Caroline out to the ranch in Montana while you clean up this mess? We'd be happy to take her in."

Martin's brows shot up and he sat back in his chair. "I didn't even think about it but that's a great idea. Getting her out of the line of fire would help immensely. Assuming she'd leave the worm, of course. Actually what I was going to ask was if you could help me with some of your law enforcement and government connections. I'll talk to Bruce this weekend and tell him I know everything. I'll get him to surrender to authorities and make him come clean. I'm hoping your friends can keep this from becoming a circus."

Travis didn't want to raise his friend's hopes. "I have to be honest here. I know a few people but I don't have the kind of influence that's going to get Bruce a deal."

Martin leaned forward, his features hardening. "He doesn't deserve a deal. He's been lying to me for months and maybe even longer. No, I just don't want this to end up on the front page of the newspapers. I'd like to avoid making a splash if only for Caro's sake. As for what the authorities do with Bruce, well, as far as I'm concerned they can throw the book at him."

"You're not going to come out of this smelling like a rose either, my friend. People are going to think you were a part of this."

"People can say whatever the hell they want." Martin finally sat back, his shoulders relaxing. "I've already made more money than most people in a hundred lifetimes. I do what I do because it's challenging but if I can't do it anymore then I'll find something new. Frankly I want to clean house and Bruce is going out with the trash. If he brings me down with him then so be it."

"You're saying you'd be fine if you had to close your fund?" Travis queried. "I find that hard to believe. You love what you do."

"I can love something else just as much," Martin countered, draining the whiskey from the highball glass. "I'm old enough to know that a career can't be your whole damn life. You need family and friends too. It's some advice you might want to embrace."

Martin had never bothered with subtlety and today was no exception.

"I'm trying but the lady is hard to convince," Travis laughed.

The anger and frustration had fallen away from Martin and now his eyes twinkled with mirth. "Since when have you had a problem with the female sex? Don't tell me this one's immune to the famous Anderson charm?"

Travis's cheeks grew warm as Martin roared with laughter, turning a few heads in the bar. "Aubrey is...different. It's not about sex. It's more than that."

Smiling widely, Martin signaled to the waitress for another round. "I was beginning to think I'd never see the day that you would fall but it's finally here. You're in love."

For the first time in my life.

"I'm not sure Aubrey is in love with me. She's several years younger than I am so I'm trying to take things slowly."

Glacially.

Travis couldn't remember the last time he'd waited as long to make love to a woman as he had with Aubrey but she was more than worth it. If she wanted to wait another month or two, or longer, he'd do it.

With blue balls.

"If she's the one then you have the rest of your lives together. No sense rushing things," Martin agreed, accepting a new whiskey from the waitress. "She seems like a lovely girl. How did you meet?"

Travis smiled grimly at the memory. "I saved her life. She was being held captive by her sister's stalker. Luckily we got to both of them in time. Gigi, her sister, persuaded Aubrey to move to Montana so they could be close to one another. I hired her as my assistant six months ago. She's damn good at her job."

Quirking an eyebrow, Martin sipped at his drink. "You're dating your assistant? What if this doesn't work? Have you thought about that?"

Only every day.

Aubrey was running him around in circles, leading him by the nose.

It was actually funny when Travis thought about it. Older, wiser, more sophisticated women had tried to land him but one look at Aubrey and he'd fallen like a ton of bricks. She preferred blue jeans over silk, and beer to champagne. She liked riding horses instead of limousines, and baking cookies with his mother instead of tea with society friends. She could talk about country music, Beethoven, fine literature, and Monty Python.

They were perfect for each other.

She was more than just beautiful although by any standard

she was gorgeous. With her long dark hair, golden skin, and generous curves she made Travis's mouth water whenever they were together. But it was her kind heart and generous nature that had truly captured him. Unlike so many women of his acquaintance she cared about others as much as she did about herself.

"It took a couple of months just to get her to go out with me. I made a deal with her that if the relationship didn't work out then I would find her a job at any of our offices all over the world. I assured her she wouldn't lose out."

"Smart. So she's giving you a run for your money, huh? Well, don't be too discouraged. All the best ones do. I could tell you a tale or two about when I was courting Donna."

Travis had already heard a few stories. Martin had chased her until she finally let him catch her. They'd been together happily for decades until her death three years ago. Martin was now married to Alana, a woman in her late forties, who enjoyed the finer things in life.

"I just hope she has a good time this weekend." Travis drained his whiskey and slapped the glass back onto the table. "We've been burning the candle at both ends on the new mine contracts so we both need a few days off to relax."

"You'll get it here."

Out of the corner of Travis's eye, he could see a smiling man making his way through the bar and to their table. Martin stood and grinned, slapping the newcomer on the back.

"Tom! When did you get in?"

Travis had met Tom Lovell several times and had always found the man friendly and easy to be around. He came from old money but now did mostly real estate and stock deals.

"Just a few minutes ago. I haven't even checked in yet but I saw you two sitting here and had to come by and say hello. Happy birthday, Martin."

"Another year older. Why don't you join us for a drink?"

"Wish I could but I need to check in with the office. Travis, I haven't seen you in months. How's the family? I heard your brothers are getting married."

"That's true," Travis chuckled. "Jason and West have been saddled. How about you, my friend?"

Tom smiled and rebuttoned his suit jacket, smoothing down the lapel. "Let's just say I'm keeping my options open. I like my freedom. Just like you, Travis."

"Are you sure you won't join us?" Martin asked.

"I really can't but I'll see you at the party tonight. Tell Caroline to save a dance or two for me."

"Will do."

Tom exited the bar leaving Martin and Travis alone again. Martin settled back into his chair with a relaxed sigh.

"That's the best part of the weekend. Spending time with friends I haven't seen in too long." Martin raised his glass. "To old friends."

Travis lifted his whiskey in salute. "To old friends. I'm glad I could be here for the party and for your birthday."

Martin glanced at his watch and grimaced. "I need to make a call to the West coast. Listen, I appreciate any help you can give me on that business matter. If you can't, I understand that too. Either way, this shit is going to get cleared up one way or another."

Both men stood and Martin tossed a hundred dollar bill on

the table before Travis could even get his wallet open. Typical.

"When are you going to talk to Bruce?"

"Before the party tonight. I won't put this off another day."

All that animosity ought to make for an interesting atmosphere this evening. Travis made a mental note to give Bruce Livingston a wide berth tonight. After talking to Martin, the man's mood wouldn't be a positive one.

Martin strode out of the bar and headed for the elevators while Travis sauntered to the resort gift shop on the other side of the lobby. Aubrey had seemed so tense earlier perhaps a little gift might make her smile. Something funny that would make her laugh. These days making her happy was all he wanted to do. He could only hope and pray he was succeeding because women like Aubrey Grayson didn't come around in a man's life very often.

Losing at the game of love? Not an option.

Chapter Three

THE CHAMPAGNE FLOWED as the band played an old Gershwin tune, the music carrying all the way out onto the open terrace of the luxurious hotel ballroom where Aubrey was currently getting a breath of fresh air. The main room was sprawling with marble floors and crystal chandeliers but she'd still become overcome with the cloying aroma of perfume. After she'd sneezed several times Travis had insisted on bringing her out here for a lungful of unpolluted oxygen and she'd gratefully accepted.

"Is this better?" he asked, his brows pulled down in concern. "You were looking a little green in there."

Aubrey took a slow, deep breath before answering. "Much. I don't mind perfume but it was like a cloud hanging over our heads in there. I think it was the mixture of all the scents, frankly. Strong floral and musk shouldn't be combined with apples and hay."

Travis smiled, showing off that dimple in his right cheek. He looked devastatingly handsome in his well-cut black tuxedo, tailored to perfection. She preferred him in blue jeans and a flannel button-down thrown over a white t-shirt but there was definitely something about a man in a suit…something hot and sexy. But then Travis couldn't have been unattractive if he tried. He had that undefinable something that drove women crazy whether they were eight or eighty. Maybe it was his charm, or his intelligence, or the way he filled out his torn blue jeans. Whatever it was he had it in spades.

"I like your perfume." He leaned down and nudged his nose along her bare shoulder sending a frisson of awareness up her spine and down to her toes. She had to concentrate to keep her knees from shaking at his nearness. "Not heavy. Not sweet. Just perfect."

Feeling the heat rise in her cheeks, she gave him a shaky laugh. "I'm not wearing any perfume. That's just soap and lotion. I was afraid the bottle might break in my suitcase and make a stinky mess."

"I doubt I'd ever describe you as stinky but you do smell good. Are you having any fun? I know my friends can be a little overwhelming when you first meet them."

"Are they all your friends?"

She'd been introduced to some lovely people so far this evening but she'd also met a few that she couldn't imagine Travis spending five minutes with.

"No, and I think you knew that before you asked the question," Travis chuckled as he slid his hands around her middle and tugged her back to his front. Aubrey relaxed in his embrace letting the tension of the party fall away. Simply enjoying the peace, she listened to the hypnotic rhythm of the waves lapping at the sugar white sand. Moonbeams danced on the surface of the water but shrouded the homes and trees in shadow as if protecting a deep, dark secret. "In fact most of these people could only be called acquaintances. I'm here for Martin this weekend and he is a friend."

"I liked him. He seems like a nice man."

"He is a nice man, one of the best. He liked you too by the way. Said I was a lucky man but then I knew that."

Pressing a kiss to her temple, Aubrey felt his warm breath on her cheek. She closed her eyes and savored the sensation of feeling completely and totally safe within his strong arms. It wasn't smart to get used to this but every now and then she allowed herself to revel in the pure pleasure of just being close to him. His fingers spread over her abdomen heating the skin through the thin fabric.

His lips skimmed her temple, his warm breath a caress against her cheek. She was as helpless as a kitten when it came to this man's advances. "This dress is fantastic. You're amazingly talented. I wish you would let me help you, sweetheart. You could set up your own business."

Tonight she was wearing a special gown she'd designed just for this occasion. At one point in her life she'd dreamed of becoming an apparel designer but quickly realized that being practical paid the rent. Luckily it was a handy skill for nights like this where she wanted to blend in with the wealthy elite.

The full-length white silk dress with skinny spaghetti straps holding up the bodice boasted a slit up the side to the top of Aubrey's thigh showing a generous amount of leg. The gown made her feel a little glamorous and she desperately needed the ego boost this evening as women dripping in diamonds flirted with Travis hoping to simply get one of his special smiles. Most of them had looked her up and down dismissively before pressing closer to him in a ploy to show off their bountiful assets. She had managed to ignore most of their high school games but she couldn't deny it was better when it was just the two of them.

Aubrey stiffened in his arms, hating that he'd brought up the sensitive subject again. They'd had this discussion before early in their working relationship. After only working with him for a few weeks she'd come into the office wearing a softly tailored pink skirt and jacket. He'd complimented her and then tried to guess the designer which had only made her laugh out loud. Assistants didn't make enough money to buy fancy duds and she didn't hesitate to point that out to Travis much to his chagrin. Eventually she'd admitted it was her own creation and he'd been impressed enough to want to discuss helping her get into the design business. She'd assumed he was simply being polite.

By the time he'd convinced her he was completely serious they'd begun seeing each other. There was no way she was going to let her boyfriend and soon to be lover shell out money to start her in business. It smacked of…payment for services rendered and she'd told him so straight out finally getting him to drop the idea.

Now he was doing it again.

"No," she said firmly. "I told you why I can't do it."

She felt his heavy sigh and knew the conversation wasn't over yet. "You shouldn't care what people think. We'll know the truth and that's all that matters."

"Bullshit." The word popped out before she could stop it but she did know better. "People with money and power always say that what others think don't matter because it doesn't matter to them. To regular people? Those things matter, Travis. It matters what people think about me. Maybe I'm shallow but I don't want to be known as a woman who slept her way into a job."

Travis was a good man and he was always trying to help her or care for her in some way but she'd been standing on her own two feet for a long time now. She wasn't a princess that needed rescuing.

"No one would ever say that about you."

"Oh, really? Are you sure? From what I've seen of your friends and business partners in the last five months they'd love to rip me to shreds. They're like coyotes that prey on the weakest antelope."

"I sure as hell wouldn't call you weak either. You scare the living shit out of me."

Travis was laughing and even Aubrey had to relax and let her lips curve into a smile. The women he'd dated before her were as different as day to night. She often wondered what he saw in her.

Aubrey leaned against his chest, his heart beating under her cheek as her gaze scanned the crowd in the ballroom. "I think I'm going to run to the ladies' room."

"I'll get you a fresh drink. Meet me at the bar."

Aubrey tucked her tiny clutch purse under her arm and headed for the dim alcove just inside the entrance to the ballroom. Once inside the restroom she quickly repaired her makeup and applied a fresh coat of lip gloss before running her fingers through her long, thick hair that had a tendency to curl in the humidity. Sighing at her reflection, she shoved everything back in her purse and zipped it shut. The trip to the ladies' room had only been a distraction anyway to keep the evening happy and light. She didn't want to ruin the party by having a disagreement with Travis no matter how innocuous.

Pushing on the door, it swung open and in her haste to rejoin Travis she ran right into another body, dropping her purse onto the marble floor. She immediately apologized and reached down but a masculine hand beat her to it, holding it out. Her breath caught in her throat and she had to forcibly straighten her knees to keep them from giving out. She took the purse from him with nerveless fingers trying to make sense of what this man was doing standing in front of her. It had been years but not nearly long enough.

Bruce Livingston.

A classmate from junior high and high school. She'd never liked him even then and now he was standing right in front of her with a triumphant smile.

Slightly paunchy around the middle and his hairline receding, his expression of sickly arrogance made her skin crawl in revulsion. He was the absolute worst person she could see tonight – or any other night for that matter.

Bruce knew all her secrets.

He knew who and what she really was.

Her fingers tightened on her clutch to keep her hands from visibly shaking as her stomach twisted violently in her abdomen. Her carefully constructed facade was about to crumble before her very eyes.

Before Travis's eyes.

Her past, long dead and buried, had clawed its way out of the grave.

Chapter Four

AUBREY NEVER HAD a chance to flee.

Bruce's hand snaked out and clamped down painfully on her arm. She'd have bruises tomorrow from his punishing grip.

"I thought it was you, Aubrey." Bruce's shark-like grin widened and a shudder of fear and revulsion ran down her spine. She was trapped. She didn't want to make a scene among this well-heeled crowd but she didn't want to stay here. "I hardly recognized you across the room. You've certainly moved up in the world hanging on Travis Anderson's arm. Does he know what a little slut you are? Or is that part of the attraction?"

Aubrey's palm itched to slap that nasty smile off of Bruce's face but instead she fisted her fingers, the nails digging into her own flesh. The pain centered her anger and kept her from hauling off and punching him in the gut.

"Let me go, Bruce."

The words came out surprisingly strong but the man didn't bat an eyelash at her command.

"Come on, babe. Don't be like that. You used to be such fun… and I'm always ready for that. Why don't we go somewhere more quiet and get to know each other again."

Acid bile had crawled up her throat and she had to swallow hard to be able to speak. "Leave me alone. We don't have anything to say to each other."

His fingers tightened and she winced, tugging at her arm. "Don't be like that. We both know that you're a little whore, Aubrey. You had quite the reputation in high school. It's a shame you and I never met up back then but we can remedy that tonight. You may have fucked practically every guy in school but I can show you what a real man is. You won't need anyone else after I've had you."

The mere suggestion of having sex with Bruce Livingston made her physically ill.

With a burst of strength, she yanked her arm away, rubbing at the livid marks his bruising grip had left behind. "Get the fuck away from me, Bruce. I'm not that girl anymore and even if I was I sure as hell wouldn't screw you. You were slime then and it looks like nothing has changed."

Bruce had been a few years ahead of Aubrey in school and kind of a jerk so she was shocked to see him at a fancy party like this one. She'd assumed he would end up selling used cars and wearing plaid suits with white shoes. Even at the most fragile moments of her life she'd had the sense to keep away from him. He had a reputation for cheating on his exams and being abusive to his girlfriends.

"You don't want to say no to me."

His left hand sported a gold wedding band and she silently pitied any woman who would have had the unfortunate luck to be married to him.

"Go back to your poor wife and leave me the hell alone."

Aubrey's voice was louder than she'd intended and a few people milling by stopped for a moment before moving on. Bruce stepped forward, crowding her personal space, and she lurched backwards only to find herself pressed up against the wall. His breath was hot with the unmistakable stench of whiskey and cigarettes. Blood pounded in her ears as his arms effectively caged her in keeping her his prisoner.

"I think you might want to be a little nicer to me, Aubrey. I'd hate to have to tell Travis what a slut you are…assuming he doesn't already know. Does he know that you're easy? That you'll do it with anyone? If he doesn't I sure as hell would love to be the one to tell him."

Heat flooded her cheeks and she opened her mouth to tell him off but he was too quick. His hand grabbed her jaw jerking her head up so they were nose to nose. Whimpering at the pain, she tried to keep her fear hidden but her vision blurred with tears.

"I'm different. I don't do that anymore."

Even to her own ears she sounded lame despite it being the God's honest truth.

Bruce laughed and leaned down so his lips were near her ear, a malodorous funk filling her nostrils and making her want to retch. She trembled and a tear escaped, running down her cheek. She'd never wanted Travis to know about her past.

Every word Bruce said was true. She had been easy in high school, sleeping with guy after guy in some mad dance to find love, affection, and acceptance. Her adoptive parents had been wonderful but she'd been haunted by the fact that her own mother couldn't love her enough to stay sober and care for her. Screwing guy after guy had been her way of coping with the rejection and pain. It had been some sort of anesthetic, numbing the anguish but never quite eradicating it.

Bruce pressed her harder against the unforgiving wall until she twisted her face away not wanting to look at him. He was so fucking satisfied with himself it was sickening.

"Right. You've changed. Sluts like you never change. You love cock, don't you? Well, I'm going to give it to you like you've never had it before."

The thought of doing anything intimate with an asshole like Bruce Livingston pushed her into action. She wasn't some shrinking violet that needed to be rescued. She was a girl from the mean streets of Chicago and she sure as hell wasn't acting like it. He might have the upper hand but that didn't mean she didn't have a play to make.

Grabbing his forearms to steady herself, she lifted her leg and drove her kneecap right into his groin, watching in satisfaction as he sucked in a breath and his eyes rolled back in his head. She shoved him away as he groaned loudly, stumbling back with his hands over his family jewels.

"You fucking cunt. I'll get you for this," Bruce spat, his face almost purple as he continued to pant, bent over and obviously hurting.

"Don't go around grabbing women, you bastard. Stay the fuck away from me."

Christ on a cracker, they'd managed to garner some definitely unwanted attention. A few people were watching them but not one person came to Bruce's aid.

His own lousy reputation must be well known.

She might be a slut but he was a douchebag, and that was far worse.

"You'll wish you hadn't done that." Bruce straightened but winced, his teeth snapping together. "I think I'll find Travis and pull him aside for a long chat. Whatever you've told him I bet it isn't the entire truth."

Game over. Her lofty perch as perfect girlfriend to Travis Anderson was about to be knocked to the ground. Bruce had always been a vindictive little shit in school and she doubted anything was different now. He would definitely find Travis and tell him everything and then probably make up more shit that wasn't even true.

"You don't scare me. Stay the hell away from me and Travis. Your threats mean nothing."

Except that they did although she thought she sounded kind of convincing.

"You're shaking you're so scared," Bruce taunted. "By the end of the night you'll be ruined. I'll make sure everyone knows about your past. Too bad you couldn't be more cooperative, Aubrey. We could have had fun together."

Turning on his heel, Bruce strode away only slightly limping from his injury. She stood there for several minutes letting her heart rate go back to normal even as guests meandered by, clearly wondering what she was doing all alone and outside the ladies' room. Finally she took a deep breath and tucked her purse under her arm.

Wiping away a stray tear, she scanned the room for Travis. She had to tell him the truth – all of it – before Bruce found him and told him his own twisted, fucked up version. At least if she did it, she could somehow explain.

It wouldn't make any difference of course. No man wanted a woman as thoroughly used and soiled as Aubrey was but keeping the secret all this time hadn't been easy. She hadn't liked hiding anything from him and it had kept them from furthering the relationship.

In and out of bed.

It would be painful and messy but it was time to come clean. She'd tell Travis her entire sordid history.

Then she'd pack her bags – she was sure he'd insist on it – and walk out of his life forever.

Pain sliced through her heart at the thought of leaving. She'd fallen for him and that had been a mistake. He'd been funny, charming, and smart. He'd treated her like a lady when she knew damn well she wasn't one. Her fairy tale world was being shredded and she only had herself to blame.

She'd tried to be perfect for him but in the end she wasn't enough. She'd never be enough. Not for him.

Chapter Five

SINCE COMING BACK from the ladies' room, Aubrey had been acting strangely. Her gaze darting around the room as if there were invisible ninjas following her, she'd barely spoken a word only gulping down a glass of champagne before Travis had drawn her onto the dance floor.

They'd made small talk and laughed but he could tell her heart wasn't in it. Her mind was a million miles away even though her body was never more than a few inches from his own. He kept his arm around her the entire evening but he could feel the slight tremble in her limbs. Her skin was pale and her lips were pressed together in a thin line. This wasn't arousal but fear.

"Baby, you can talk to me about anything, you know."

He kept his lips close to her ear so she could hear him over the band playing in the background.

Instead of looking him in the eye, her gaze fell to the floor.

"Can we go upstairs? I have a headache."

Her untouched birthday cake sat on the table in front of them. Aubrey loved chocolate but she'd barely glanced at the plate that had been slid in front of her over a half an hour ago.

Instead she'd looked around nervously clearly upset about...something.

"Of course. We've done our duty here tonight. We'll go upstairs and I'll draw you a nice, hot bath. How does that sound?"

Aubrey looked up at him but he had a feeling that she didn't really *see* him. "Wonderful. You spoil me, Travis."

"You deserve it." It felt like he was always telling her this and she didn't seem to understand that he enjoyed taking care of her and seeing her smile. She never asked for anything which only made him want to give her everything.

He heard her swift indrawn breath and she blinked a few times, her eyes shiny in the low lights. "No, I don't but I love that you think so."

"It's going to be my pleasure to convince you otherwise."

Aubrey finally looked up at him, their gazes locking. Her chin lifted as if she expected a right hook to the jaw.

"Travis, we need to talk."

In the long history of mankind, nothing good had come from those four words. Travis was about to get kicked to the curb and he didn't have a clue as to why. His heart skipped a beat or two and his abdomen tightened painfully.

There wasn't a damn thing he could do to stop this. He'd fallen hard for Aubrey and he'd thought she'd felt the same. She'd been shy and tentative but there had been a softness in her eyes that he'd taken for love. Or at least something that might turn into love.

He'd been wrong.

For perhaps the first time in his life, he'd let himself believe that she'd cared. He'd convinced himself that he was making her happy. Now he'd have a broken heart to show for it.

Because he wouldn't fucking beg her to stay although every cell in his body was screaming for him to do just that. Hell, a man had to have some dignity and he wasn't planning to lose his no matter what happened in the next few minutes.

"Of course we can talk, kitten. What do you want to talk about?"

Travis kept his tone mild as if she said things like this every day.

Her fingers played with the stem of the champagne glass. "I need to tell you something."

She wasn't making this easy for either of them. If she was dumping him it would be far kinder to just get to it and be done.

"You can tell me anything."

He was a big fat liar but what else could he say?

Her knuckles had gone white and her chest rose and fell quickly in her agitation. Whatever it was she had to tell him she clearly didn't find it pleasant.

"I probably should have told you sooner," she began, looking down at the table where her fingers gripped the edge. "But…it's just that it's hard to talk about. I've spent the last few years trying to put it behind me."

Wait. This didn't sound like a brush off. More like a confession.

Travis reached out to capture her fingers with his own. "Honey, whatever you have to tell me is going to be fine. If you don't want to tell me that's fine too."

Aubrey shook her head, her expression resolute. "No, I want to. It's been weighing on my mind every day."

He didn't like the sound of that so he squeezed her hand in encouragement, moving his chair closer to her own.

"Then I want to hear it. But the ballroom of this fine establishment probably isn't the best place to have a personal conversation. What do you think?"

Her cheeks turned rosy and she looked around as if noticing for the first time they weren't alone.

"This is not the place. How about a walk on the beach?"

Travis kept his arm wrapped around her middle as they headed for the French doors, his fingers brushing the silken ends of her long hair. Stripping off their shoes at the bottom of the staircase, they dug their toes into the sand as the sound of the waves drowned out the music wafting from the ballroom.

"So what is it that you want to tell me, kitten?"

"I need to tell you–" Aubrey broke off, her forehead crinkled. She pointed to the water lapping at the shore. "What's that?"

A dark lump was lying on the beach the water pooling around it with each pull of the tide. "I'll check but it's probably just a bag of garbage someone dumped. People these days have no respect for nature. I'll have the resort staff clean it up."

Except when Travis got a good look he could clearly see arms and legs. Something had been dumped on the beach but it wasn't trash.

"Aubrey, go upstairs."

Travis fished for the phone in his pocket intending to call 911.

"What is it?"

Now she was right next to him and could see everything he could by the sound of her sucked in breath.

"You don't listen worth a damn, woman. I said go upstairs."

Travis gently shoved her toward the resort and away from the body but she didn't budge an inch.

"Stubborn as hell," Travis growled under his breath as he took a few steps forward to get a better look. The man was lying on his back his face only half illuminated but Travis easily recognized him.

"Who is it?" Aubrey asked, her voice quivering and her arms wrapped around her torso. "Is he dead?"

Very dead. Bruce Livingston's chest was covered in blood, his face ghostly pale.

Chapter Six

TRAVIS ONCE AGAIN had to rein in his displeasure. He wasn't the most patient of men on the best days and finding a dead body – someone he knew – certainly made it one of the worst. He hadn't been a friend of Bruce Livingston but he'd never wished anything bad to happen to him.

Travis had already told his story to the first police officer on the scene but the detective who had just arrived wanted to hear it again which meant that the first recitation hadn't been recorded in any way. He couldn't help but think that West's cops would be better organized.

They were currently sequestered away from the other party guests in another hotel conference room. Travis kept his arm around Aubrey trying to comfort her in some way. She'd been pale and drawn since they'd found Bruce dead, shaking and looking close to tears. He blamed himself as he should have been a hell of a lot more forceful about sending her back upstairs but he simply hadn't known how grisly the scene was until they both were right up on it. It had been way too dark outside even with the full moon.

"Can we get you folks some coffee or water?" The detective

from the local police department waved toward a long table against the wall. Probably in his mid-forties, he had that world weary appearance that often seemed to go with a long career in law enforcement. His hairline was receding, his face was tanned and lined, and his suit slightly rumpled. "The resort staff has graciously provided some refreshments."

"Nothing for me. Aubrey?"

She shook her head as well and took a few deep breaths. "No, I'm fine. I'd like to get this over with and go up to our room."

From the look on the cops face, Travis didn't think that was going to happen any time in the near future. The dark haired man had settled in, ordering coffee and pastries while gathering Bruce's family and friends in the room next to this one. It was going to be a long night.

"My name is Detective Dan Prather and I'm now in charge of this case. Can you tell me how you came to find the deceased?"

Travis squeezed Aubrey's hand to let her know he would take these questions. "Miss Grayson and I were heading down to the beach and that's when we saw Bruce lying there."

He knew enough about cops to know to keep his answers brief and to the point. No extra details. No editorializing.

"Why were you going to the beach?"

"We wanted a quiet place to talk."

The detective's brows lifted and his lips twisted into a smirk. "Talk? May I ask what about?"

Aubrey's shoulders jerked in response to the question but Travis simply pulled her closer to his own body. "How is that relevant to the investigation, Detective?"

The man's flinty blue eyes iced over and his jaw hardened. "I'm just trying to get all the facts, Mr. Anderson. Two people at a party go out to the beach to find a quiet place to talk when they have a fifteen hundred square foot suite upstairs? That brings questions to my mind."

"We didn't want to leave the party. We wanted a few moments to talk. That's all."

The detective tapped his stubby pencil against the pad of paper. "How well did you know Mr. Livingston?"

Travis shrugged, expecting that question. "I saw him once or twice a year at parties like this one. He's the grandson in law of a good friend."

"Martin Guinness?" Travis nodded wondering how his friend was holding up. "So how would you characterize your relationship with the deceased?"

"Acquaintances," Travis answered easily. "We didn't keep in touch other than seeing each other at these events. We weren't friends if that's what you're asking."

"That is what I'm asking. So you didn't communicate in any way with Mr. Livingston? If I check his phone, your number won't be there?"

"I have no clue what will be in his phone but I've never received a call from him."

It took every bit of willpower he had to keep the sarcasm out of his tone. There was a murderer running around and this clown was acting like he and Aubrey were suspects. They had nothing to do with Bruce's death but Travis could name a few people off the top of his head that hadn't thought much of the man. He didn't like to speak ill of the dead but finding those with motive wasn't going to be a problem.

"When was the last time you saw Mr. Livingston?"

"Earlier this evening. Right after dinner. About nine or nine thirty."

The detective abruptly swung his attention to Aubrey. "What about you Miss Grayson? What time did you last see Mr. Livingston?"

Her hands were twisted together in her lap, the knuckles white. "I–I guess it would have been a little later. About ten thirty."

Travis could feel the tension vibrating through Aubrey's body.

"And where did you see him?"

"Out–Outside the ladies' room."

Her voice quivered and Travis wanted to pick her up and cuddle her to his chest. Clearly she was terrified of the police. She'd had a very different upbringing in Chicago than he'd had in Montana. Perhaps her memories of law enforcement weren't as positive as his own.

"Did you speak to him, Miss Grayson?" the detective pressed, his lips a straight line. Travis didn't like the way the man was looking at Aubrey.

"She doesn't even know–" began Travis but she shushed him, shaking her head.

"Yes, I did speak to him but only for a moment."

She hadn't mentioned anything about it when she'd rejoined him. As shy as she was there was no way Aubrey had approached Bruce. He had to have talked to her first.

"And what did you talk about?"

That was a really good question. One that Travis wanted answered as well. Bruce had considered himself something of a ladies man and Travis had an idea of what might have transpired between them.

More trembling and then Aubrey took a deep breath. "He recognized me across the room. We went to school together in Chicago."

Travis froze and stared down at the beautiful woman next to him. "You knew him?"

Nodding, she placed her hand on his. "That's one of the things I wanted to tell you. We went to the same junior high and high school."

"Did you date Mr. Livingston, Miss Grayson?" the detective asked, obviously trying to get their attention back on him.

Aubrey wrinkled her nose at the suggestion. "No! I barely knew him. He was two years ahead of me but I knew of him I guess you could say. But I'm not sure we ever even spoke to one another although we had some mutual…friends."

Prather's gaze flickered to Travis and then back to Aubrey. "We have witnesses that place you and Mr. Livingston in the alcove outside the ladies room arguing about an hour before his body was found. Is that true?"

Of course it wasn't true. Eye witness accounts were notoriously faulty and should never be relied upon.

Sagging against him, her lips turned down in what looked like defeat.

"Yes. Yes, it is true."

✦   ✦   ✦

AUBREY HAD MANAGED to shock Travis, the unshakable man.

She hadn't wanted him to hear about Bruce and her past...this way. Her mind raced as she tried to find a way to explain the situation without spilling her guts about things that didn't – or shouldn't – matter. Her past was none of the detective's business.

But she better think fast because it was obvious she was a suspect.

"What did you argue about Miss Grayson? Specifically, please."

Her nails dug into her palms and her heart pounded against her ribs. It was her worst nightmare come to life.

"Bruce...Mr. Livingston, I mean, made a pass at me and I declined."

It was the truth although she'd left out the ugly backstory.

"And he was angry about that?"

"Yes. Very angry. He grabbed my arm."

She held up her arm to show off the already visible bruises. Travis's grip tightened on her shoulder and she could feel the rage radiating off of him.

"I'd like our crime lab guys to get a picture of those bruises if you don't mind. So what happened after that?"

"He pushed me against a wall and I kneed him in the balls. He said some nasty words and I walked away. That's it."

"Good for you," Travis approved. "Everyone knows what Bruce was like. Talk to anyone, Detective, they'll tell you that he could be handsy and ignore the boundaries of good taste. I doubt

Aubrey was the first woman to have to fight him off."

Awash in guilt that Travis was defending her when he didn't know the entire story, she avoided meeting his gaze, looking intently over the detectives shoulder although there wasn't really anything to see.

"Did anything else happen, Miss Grayson?" Detective Prather didn't acknowledge Travis's commentary in any way. "Did Mr. Livingston have any reason, based on your previous relationship, to believe you'd have sex with him?"

"No!" Hell, she wasn't even having sex with the man sitting next to her and she adored him. "He had absolutely no reason to think that except his own ego. He wasn't the nicest person in school and apparently he didn't change much. I kept my distance then."

"Did you know he was going to be here at the party tonight?" Prather pressed, his eyes narrowed as if he was trying to see through her. He thought she was hiding something. She was of course but not what he believed.

"Again, no," she said firmly, meeting his gaze directly. "I assumed I didn't know anyone here this weekend."

"You didn't know he had married Martin Guinness's granddaughter?"

Aubrey exhaled slowly hanging onto her temper by a thread. She understood why she was being questioned but the interview had made a frightening turn.

"Detective," Travis cut in smoothly. "We want to help you but I'm not sure where you're going with this line of questioning."

Prather smiled but it didn't reach his eyes. "It's my job to cover all the bases, Mr. Anderson. If Miss Grayson and the deceased had any prior relationship I'd like to know about it."

"She told you they didn't," Travis shot back. "Are we done here? Miss Grayson has had a rather trying evening. Seeing a dead body and all."

The sarcasm in his tone was unmistakable and the detective clearly wasn't amused.

"For now," Prather conceded, snapping his notebook closed. "Stay close as I'm sure I'll need to talk to you again. I appreciate your…cooperation."

Travis stood and gathered her close, his arm a reassuring weight around her waist. "One of your men took my cell number so you can get in touch with us. Come on, Aubrey. You need to rest."

Blood still pounding in her ears, she allowed Travis to lead her down the hall and into an elevator. As the doors glided shut, he pressed a kiss to her temple and ran his fingers through her hair.

"A hot bath and a strong drink is what we both need. Then I think you and I need to have that talk."

Everything she'd feared since meeting Travis was coming true. She couldn't hide what she was any longer and frankly she didn't want to. She was exhausted keeping up the charade.

She'd tell him everything.

Chapter Seven

AUBREY SIPPED AT the brandy, its fire warming up her belly and making her fingers and toes tingle. She'd soaked in the bathtub until she was wrinkled like a prune before scrubbing off her makeup and changing into a pair of sweatpants and t-shirt. If she was going to bare her soul to Travis then she might as well be comfortable. It wasn't like they were going to be a couple by the time she was finished.

He'd be polite and understanding, of course. That was the kind of man he was, but he'd end the relationship just the same. He'd tell her that perhaps things weren't going to work out between them and then he'd find her another job somewhere in the Anderson holdings.

Like Magellan, she'd be history.

But then she'd never expected anything different. It had only happened sooner than she'd predicted.

She was sitting on the loveseat in the bedroom, her legs curled under her, staring at the television that was currently muted. Anything to avoid looking him in the eye and confessing a multitude of sins.

He sat down next to her and waited, not saying a word, letting her gather her thoughts once again. Finally when she couldn't take the silence any longer, she broke.

"I never wanted to tell you."

A gentle smile played around his well-shaped lips. "Clearly. Although I must tell you that unless you've killed a homeless man or cheated people in a Ponzi scheme, everything is going to be fine. Hell, even then you probably had a good reason."

It was her turn to smile even at a shit moment like this. "I've never killed or cheated anyone."

"Then this can't be that bad, kitten. Trust me a little and tell me."

She did trust him. More than she had anyone in her life. Travis Anderson was a good man, one of the best, but she was asking too much of him to not care that the woman in his life had been around the block dozens of times.

Slut. Whore. Easy. Tramp.

That's what she'd been called by the other girls in school. Those catty ones who looked down at her and made sure she didn't get invited to certain parties. They'd made her school years hell and even now all this time later those eager twins – guilt and shame – couldn't leave her in peace. She hadn't known it as a naive teenager but she knew it now...

A person has to live every day with the decisions they make. Good or bad.

"You know I was in foster care and then I was adopted," she began, figuring she should start at the beginning. "My family was good to me but I had a lot of baggage. Things I had a hard time dealing with."

Travis ran a finger across her jaw, tender and slow. "Did

Bruce hurt you back then, sweetheart?"

Her throat swelled with emotion and she shook her head, forcing the words out. "No. It was the truth when I said I barely knew him. But I'll get to him in a minute, okay?"

She took his silence as agreement and pushed forward, afraid that if she paused she'd lose what little courage she'd managed to scrape together.

"As I said, I had a lot of baggage. Most of it was about my mother and wondering how a parent couldn't love and care for their children. It made me feel unworthy of anyone loving me. Let's face it, if a parent can't love you, then what's the chances of anyone else loving you?"

"That's not true—" he protested but she pressed her fingers to his lips.

"I know that now but I didn't feel that then. Please let me tell this before I lose my nerve."

He nodded but both his hands came up to wrap around her own, warm and caring and so needed. She would miss his touch when she left tonight. She couldn't stay around to see the distaste on his face when she was done telling her story.

"I hungered for affection. My adoptive parents were sweet but not demonstrative. I'd never been held or cuddled as a child and by the time I became a teenager I wanted it so badly. That's when things sort of went south."

Aubrey had to steady her voice, her entire body shaking with emotion. Reliving the past was her least favorite thing to do and here she was doing it. Shame choked her and she had to swallow hard to be able to continue.

"I realized I could get attention from boys. They liked the

way I looked and I began to flirt with them. It made me feel better about myself that they'd call me or ask me out. But like a junkie, that soon wasn't enough. When I was fifteen I lost my virginity in the backseat of a Ford Taurus near the lake to a football player." She closed her eyes in misery, tears welling up despite her desperate attempt to keep them at bay. "The next weekend I had sex with one of his teammates. And the next weekend another. Before too long I had plenty of guys paying attention to me. As long as I gave them what they wanted they gave me what my twisted-up brain had convinced me was love and affection. I used sex to numb the pain of my mother reject-ing me. I lost track of the number of guys I slept with."

Travis was silent although his grip had tightened. Aubrey didn't dare look up to see the expression of disgust on his face. She didn't think she could bear it.

"I was the school slut. Basically, I'd sleep with any guy that said I was pretty. I did that until senior year when one of the few girlfriends I had got pregnant. It sort of snapped me back to reality and I straightened out. But it was too late, really. I was shunned by most kids in my school even though I lived like a nun the rest of that school year. I was a whore and no one was ever going to let me forget it."

She moved her legs restlessly, her body filled with a pain so acute it almost took her breath away.

"And tonight Bruce reminded me of what I really am. I'd almost forgotten. I've spent the last ten years trying to run from it but I realize that's never going to happen. I wanted to be perfect for you so badly, Travis. I wanted to be the kind of woman you could care about, but the fact is I'm still that trashy lay from Chicago. I'm so fucking sorry that I didn't tell you in the beginning. I really am. I could have saved both of us all of this."

Travis had levered up from the loveseat and begun to pace the room, back and forth, as if he was pondering the secrets of the universe. Aubrey said nothing, too exhausted from her confessions to say much more. In reality all she wanted to do was crawl away and curl up in the fetal position for the next several days. A dreamless sleep was the only thing that would stop the hurt from her shattered heart.

He finally stopped, standing in front of her, but she tried to keep her gaze on his shoes. Tugging at his bow tie, he tossed it onto the arm of a chair with a heavy sigh, along with his jacket.

"Aubrey, look at me."

Deep and commanding, she found herself obeying his voice even though it was difficult to see him through her tears. She'd never wanted it to come to this.

"I am so fucking angry right now and I'm trying to keep myself under control."

"I'm sorry–" she began but he reached down and pressed a finger over her lips, getting on his knees so they were eye to eye.

"I'm not angry with you so stop apologizing. You don't have a damn thing to apologize for, kitten, although it sounds like you don't believe that. But this talk between us is apparently long overdue." He leaned forward, their noses almost touching. "And by the way, if you ever call yourself a slut or a whore again you're going to find yourself over my knee getting a very unpleasant spanking. I won't allow you to denigrate yourself in any way. Am I understood?"

No, she didn't understand in the least. She'd slept around. She didn't know how many guys she'd had sex with. She'd lost count.

"But–"

His lips crashed into hers effectively silencing her, and they both tumbled back onto the small sofa, their bodies pressed together. When he lifted his head his expression was a mask of control.

"I mean it. Don't ever speak of yourself that way again. I don't care if you've slept with the entire NFL. Just fucking stop it. I won't tolerate it."

More tears welled up in her eyes and his face softened, pulling her onto his lap.

"Is that what you've been torturing yourself with all this time? Is this the thing that's been holding you back these last months? This mistaken notion that somehow you're not good enough?"

She wasn't nearly good enough.

"You're not listening to me–"

"Stop it," Travis exploded, his cheeks turning ruddy with anger. "I fucking mean it. Stop it. I don't give a shit, Aubrey. I don't care how many guys you've had sex with. Do you care how many women I've had sex with?"

"Well…no…not really, but you're missing the point."

His fingers dug into her shoulders, turning her so she had to look into his eyes. "I don't think I am, sweetness. If you had been a guy you would have been a high school hero, but you were a girl. And girls aren't supposed to want sex or enjoy it, right? Isn't that what this is all about? Some stupid societal double standard? None of this matters."

"But…"

He was confusing her and her head already pounded from the worrying and the crying. Since her run-in with Bruce she'd felt like hell.

"But what? Tell me why it's different for you than for me."

"It just is," she answered lamely, her heart rate beginning to return to normal. "And you know it is."

"Maybe to a bunch of closed-minded kids who see the world as black and white, but I hope I've moved past that. Shit, if it's okay for a guy to have sex and it isn't for a girl, well, who the hell is he supposed to have sex with, anyway? Those nosy busybodies didn't think that one through, did they? The whole thing is just stupid."

He didn't care. Really. Truly. At least she wanted to believe that. His words sounded so amazingly wonderful. For the first time in a long time she felt something akin to hope, although she was probably a fool for even entertaining the notion.

"I–I slept with a lot of guys, Travis. A lot."

His right brow inched up and his fingers captured her chin, rubbing along the jawline and sending shivers down her spine.

"You said that already. But you didn't murder or cheat anyone, right? So I'm not sure what you feel guilty about, baby. I sure as shit haven't been a saint either. Should I start confessing my sins?"

"No!" Aubrey pressed her fingers against his lips in alarm. The last thing she wanted to hear about was his sexual exploits before her. She already had an inferiority complex and that wouldn't help it. "I think that's best left in the past."

"But yours isn't?" he pressed. "I never expected a virgin, kitten, and I sure don't deserve one considering my past. I'm just sorry that Bruce brought this all up again. What did he say to you?"

Aubrey sighed and closed her eyes for a moment, reliving the ugly scene. She hated to tell Travis about it but he had that determined look in her eye she'd come to know so well. She'd never hear the end of it until she told him every dirty detail.

"He threatened me." Travis waited quietly for her to continue but she could see the muscle working in his jaw. He was already pissed as hell and she hadn't even told him the worst part. "He said that if I didn't have sex with him he'd tell you all about my past."

"He tried to make you ashamed of having sex? Of enjoying it? Fucking asshole."

Travis's voice came out as a hiss, anger etched in every line of his face. He was livid. But he still didn't understand what she'd been inarticulately trying to tell him.

"It's not…well…I didn't…it's just…"

Telling him this part was almost worse.

"You're not defending him, are you? Bruce is a well-known bastard so I'm not surprised he did it, honestly. I'm just sorry that you got caught up in all this. He hates me and I'm sure no matter what you did he was looking forward to telling something he thought was going to upset me. But sweetheart, make no mistake, I don't care about your past. All I care about is the present and the future."

Aubrey was still having trouble wrapping her mind around the fact that she'd told Travis her deepest, darkest secret and he hadn't sent her packing.

"I'm certainly not defending him. He is a douche. But you said that I was ashamed of enjoying sex and that's not it at all. That's not why I'm ashamed."

Frowning, Travis ran his hands up and down her arms, sending warmth into her cold extremities.

"Then what are you ashamed of, baby?"

"That I kept doing it even though I didn't like it. I really never enjoyed it. I don't think that I can."

The final confession. She was a slut who didn't care for sex. Ironic as hell.

Now he knew how screwed up she truly was.

Chapter Eight

THE ENTIRE SITUATION was completely screwed up.

His Aubrey actually thought he'd care that she'd been free with her favors when she was younger. He didn't care what she'd done before as long as she was only his from now on. But her other confession that she didn't like sex made him sad. She thought there was something wrong with her.

There wasn't a damn thing wrong with her.

He'd kissed this woman. Caressed her soft skin and traced her curves with his hands. He'd felt her tremble in his arms and had smelled her arousal. She wasn't frigid or unresponsive. She might not be a virgin but she sounded...unawakened.

"Sweetheart, I think we need to talk about this a little bit. Are you saying you don't want to have sex with me? Because it's okay if you don't."

What was a lifetime of blue balls anyway?

Her eyes flew open and she shook her head vehemently. "But I do. Really." A blush crawled up her neck and face as she realized what she'd said. His heart pounded against his ribcage and his blood pressure hitched up several points. She was adorable. "I'm attracted to you. Honestly."

"That's good to hear, baby. Really good. But you don't expect to enjoy it, is that why you're trying to say?"

She looked relieved and nodded. "Exactly. I don't want you to think it's your fault because it's not."

"Hmmm…that's good to know."

She was serious. She thought she wasn't capable of great passion.

"Are you sure it doesn't make any difference?"

Her question was hesitant, almost fearful, and he splayed his hand on her lower back to pull her a little closer to him.

"I don't care about your past and I don't care what happened with other men. The only thing that matters is you and me. I hope you feel the same way."

He should have anticipated them but he hadn't, so he was caught off guard when her beautiful brown eyes filled with tears and they began to slide down her creamy cheeks, a few dropping on his shirt. Her whole body was shaking like a leaf on a windy autumn day.

"I was so worried. I thought you'd kick me out." Aubrey buried her head in his chest and he wrapped his arms around her, tightly rocking her back and forth as if she were a child. She hadn't received enough love and adoration and he promised right then and there to rectify that situation. He'd shower her with affection and attention until she screamed for mercy.

"If I kicked you out then I'd have to kick my own ass out as well, kitten. I've done a bunch of things I'm not proud of, most of them in my youth, thankfully. Give yourself a break. No one is perfect."

"You are," she sniffled as he handed her a handkerchief from his pocket.

The sentiment was sweet but terribly misguided. He was nothing to write home about, his flaws on clear display.

"Far from it. Honestly, I'm a mess," he chuckled. "I'm nowhere near perfect as you should well know. You work for me, after all. If that isn't enough we can give my sister and brothers a call. They'll be happy to tell you how pointless my existence on this earth is. In fact, they love reminding me of that whenever we're together."

Aubrey rolled her eyes as she dabbed at her nose. "I do work for you and you forget that I've seen all the lovesick women parading in and out of your life. There's something about you that women adore, Travis."

"Yeah, my money," he snorted. "Don't make the mistake of thinking it's any more than that. I attract a certain type of lady that believes size matters. As in the size of my bank account. They don't usually care much about me personally."

"You don't think I'm like that, do you?"

Biting her lip, her eyes were starting to fill with more tears. He'd screwed up again.

"Of course not." His arms tightened around her and he pressed his face to her fragrant tresses. "I know you like me for me and that's one of the big reasons we're together. You don't care how much money I have or where we eat dinner, what parties we attend. You'd much rather hang around my house and watch television or ride horses. You came here this weekend for me, not for you."

"You could tell that? I guess I'm just not a glamour type girl."

"Thank God, because that's what I prefer too. I do parties like this because of social commitments and good friends, but honestly I'd just rather take you out for a moonlit horseback ride next to the lake. I'd lay out a blanket and a picnic and we could make out under the stars."

From her brilliant smile it appeared she really liked that idea but then her lips turned down in sadness.

"I'd like nothing better but I have to get through this week-end first. That detective suspects me and let's face it. I have a motive. A good one."

A motive she hadn't told the cop about, which worried Travis. If the detective found out about it on his own then Aubrey would be under even more suspicion.

"I wish you had been honest about Bruce's blackmail but I understand why you weren't. Although you should have known I wouldn't care about your past. It hurts to think that you thought me that self-righteous and judgmental, baby."

She tried to move from his lap but he held her fast. "It wasn't that I thought you were like that but...I just thought you wouldn't want...a used girlfriend."

Travis sighed with frustration. "You're not a car, you're a woman. A beautiful, sexy, amazing woman and it never occurred to me that I was the first man to realize it. I'm sure you've had many boyfriends through the years."

She opened her mouth to say something, then seemed to think better of it. "That's another discussion but not for tonight. Right now all I can think of is that Bruce is dead and Prather thinks I did it."

"He hasn't talked to everyone yet," Travis laughed, thinking about the guests this weekend. "Once he does he'll see that there is no shortage of people that had motive to kill Bruce. Many of them much stronger than yours. The man was an asshole and pretty much everybody knew it. He didn't bother to hide it."

"Will he talk to everyone? Or will he just find a convenient scapegoat – namely me – and close the case?"

Her voice trembled with fear and he couldn't stand the thought of her being so terrified. "I'm not going to let anything happen to you. I'll get Shane out here and if I have to find the real killer myself, I damn well will. No one is going to railroad you into a murder charge on my watch."

"Shane? How can he help?"

Aubrey didn't know his cousin's background.

"He's an attorney. A damn good one too, which is important in business dealings. He's not a member of the bar here in Florida but he does know the law. I'll give him a call."

Shoving her hair back from her face, Aubrey appeared slightly dazed. "This day has been so strange. First Bruce threatens me, then he ends up dead, and now I've told you my biggest secret. And you don't seem to care."

He'd told her several times already, but he had a feeling she was going to have to hear it many more times before she believed deep in her heart.

"I don't care. I'm not going to judge you for what you've done. Hell, with everything that you've been through your reaction doesn't seem all that extreme. Some people might have turned to drugs or crime."

A smile bloomed on her beautiful face and his heart skipped a few beats. "Did I forget to mention the multi-million dollar crime syndicate I'm the head of?"

He captured her lips in a long, hot kiss that left them both breathless. "Baby, make me an offer I can't refuse."

"How about you shower up and I'll rub your shoulders. Your forehead has those lines again so I know you're feeling tense."

Aubrey always seemed to know when he was feeling stressed just by looking at his expressions. He didn't know how she did it but she was never wrong.

"I'm worried about Martin," he admitted. "He has a powerful motive for murder and the police are bound to find out about it."

"Do you think he did it?" Aubrey asked, her voice soft and tentative.

"No, but as you pointed out that won't stop the police from ripping apart someone's life. I think it might be a good idea to do a little investigating on our own. I don't know much about the local law enforcement, but you made a good point earlier about placing too much trust there. We need to take control of this situation if we want to stay on top of it."

His mind was moving in fast forward, making a list of things to be done and people to call.

"At this point I'm grateful for any help I can get," Aubrey sighed. "I'm not too proud to admit that I'm scared. I didn't like Bruce but I didn't want him dead."

"There are dozens of people who did and we'll go through them with a fine-tooth comb. We'll find who really did this and clear your name once and for all."

If it was the last thing he'd do, Travis would help Aubrey put the past behind her and move forward.

With him.

Chapter Nine

AUBREY COULDN'T SLEEP. She'd tossed and turned for the last hour, wide awake, her head spinning with the events of the evening. She needed a shot of whiskey or maybe a sleeping pill. As it stood now she'd be up all night.

Throwing back the covers she padded into the bathroom, rummaging through her toiletry case for a few ibuprofen with the added sleep medication. She'd kill her headache and her sleeplessness in one shot. She tossed back two tablets with a glass of water and opened the bathroom door only to smack into a hard wall of warm, muscular man.

"Shit! You scared me."

She sagged against the doorframe, her hand on her racing heart, trying to catch her breath. For a moment she'd been stuck in one of the horror movies she loved to watch. Add in a killer on the loose and she'd almost fainted with fright.

"I didn't mean to." Travis reached for her and she let him tug her into his safe embrace. Suddenly serial killers and crazed clowns didn't seem so scary. "I heard you moving around and I was worried."

"I was quiet. How did you hear me? I just came in here to

take something to help me sleep. I can't turn my mind off."

Aubrey reached into her case and rattled the bottle of pills.

"It will take a while for those to kick in, but maybe I can help you relax like you helped me. Wait here."

She was glad the shoulder massage had relaxed him enough that he was able to get some rest, but if his plan was to return the favor it wouldn't work. His big, strong hands on her body weren't going to relax her in the least. Arousal would be the more than likely outcome.

He disappeared into his bedroom and came back out with a blanket, nudging her along with short hallway to the living room area. Snagging two water bottles from the bar he led her out to the patio where they snuggled on a chaise lounge wrapped up in the blanket. Aubrey could see a scattering of stars in the deep purple night sky along with the bright moon that cast shadows over the trees and buildings.

"It's not the lake and we didn't get to ride but it's not half bad. At least it's warm."

It was perfect. The temperature had dropped enough that the blanket was welcome but not so low that she was chilled. A gentle breeze was blowing off the Gulf, bringing with it a tangy, salty aroma that soothed her overwrought senses. It was no wonder people came here to destress from the hustle and bustle of everyday life.

"It's beautiful. A different kind of beauty than Montana but still gorgeous."

She laid her head on his chest as it rose and fell steadily under her cheek. It epitomized this man – rock solid. Someone that could be depended upon. He made other men seem pale and uninteresting.

"We can come here more often if you like," he offered. "I'm always up for a beach weekend."

Did he really believe that he had to give her vacations and gifts? She once again wondered what kind of women he'd dated in the past. Were they all a bunch of mercenary bitches?

"Do you really think women only date you for your money?" she blurted, wincing as the words came out sounding much less smooth than they had in her head.

She could feel his laughter start as a rumble deep in his chest. "I know it for a fact, baby. If I dug ditches for a living I have no doubt that I'd be much less popular with the ladies."

"Not all women are like that."

"No, they aren't and I don't mean to make it sound like they are. I've dated some lovely females in my life. Really smart, funny women who didn't care about the size of my wallet but there have been more than a few that were quite open about coveting my financial assets."

Those women were certifiably crazy. Travis was handsome, sexy, smart, and sweet. His money and success was such a minuscule part of who he was. Born into any other family he would have been good at whatever he'd chosen to do. If he'd been a ditch digger they would have been the best damn holes in the ground anyone had ever laid eyes on.

"You have a lot more to offer besides your money."

Travis tugged on a strand of her hair, sending arrows of arousal straight to her feminine parts.

"Like what?"

With a fingernail she traced a pattern on his chest over his t-shirt. "You're handsome. And smart. Kind of dangerous in negotiations. I actually felt sorry for that guy when we were working on the mine contracts. He wasn't in your league and he knew it."

"I doubt my girlfriends cared much about that. Not too many wanted the details of my work."

"You also have a kind heart. You're close to your family and you're very charitable. I bet that soup kitchen should have a photo of you on the wall with the words 'Our Founder' emblazoned on it even though you're always pretending the things you do for the community are no big deal. They're a big deal for the people you help. And let's not even mention the fact that you saved my life. If it weren't for you and Jason, Gigi and I would be pushing up daisies. Don't think I don't know that."

His fingers ran along her jaw and softly traced her lips, setting a thousand butterflies free in her abdomen. "You make me sound like a cross between Santa Claus and James Bond. Believe me, I have a lot of faults. Tons of them."

Like she didn't know. But they seemed insignificant when compared with his positive qualities.

"I'm your assistant. I'm well aware. You growl until you've had your first cup of coffee. You sing off key when the radio's on in your office. You're impatient with yourself when you don't live up to your own expectations and you can get lost in work to the point where you forget about the outside world. You also don't eat enough vegetables."

To her delight Travis threw back his head and laughed. "You've been monitoring my diet? That's going above and beyond, baby. It's just that junk food tastes so damn good and

Brussels sprouts taste like a grilled tennis shoe. Something went wrong in the universe there. But you missed so many other faults."

"Like what?"

"I snore," he stated with a grin. "Loudly. Like cows stir in pastures miles away. I hope you're a heavy sleeper."

She wasn't and his intimation that they would soon be sharing a bed made color rise in her cheeks.

"You might want to see a doctor about that. It can't be healthy. What else?"

"I snore because I broke my nose a few times playing football. Not much they can do. Let's see what else? Oh yeah, I'm a hot water hog. I love taking long showers and I empty the water heater, leaving none for anyone else."

That *was* kind of rude.

"Do you leave the toilet seat up? That and the hot water thing might be a deal breaker."

"After living alone for so long I sure do. Looks like this thing between us is doomed to a fiery death."

Except he was wearing a shit eating grin and not a sad face.

"Looks like it," Aubrey agreed, trying to hide her own mirth. "Too bad, but now I guess I get to work in your Paris office."

"But perhaps I could be persuaded to reform. Or maybe I could give you your own bathroom."

Aubrey giggled, delighting in his playfulness after a terrible, awful day. "It sounds like I'd need my own zip code if what you say about your snoring is true. At least I'd need my own water heater. Besides, men never really change."

"I can change, woman." Aubrey loved the growl in Travis's

tone and this time she couldn't hide her laughter. "I have worlds of change inside me. I'm the old dog that can learn new tricks, I'll have you know."

"You're not old."

His smile fell and he pushed a stray strand of hair back from her face. "I am old. Older than you anyway. Does it bother you?"

"No, and it shouldn't bother you. I haven't had much luck dating men my own age, actually. I think I'm what they call an old soul. I'd rather hang around the house with you having a quiet night than going to some loud nightclub to drink and dance."

"There is a middle ground. It doesn't have to be one or the other."

"Does it bother you that I'm young? I'm probably immature compared to most of the women you've dated."

Plain and unsophisticated too.

"You're much more mature in truth. But then in the past I dated for fun, not thinking about the future."

"Are you thinking about the future now?"

Shit, she couldn't stop herself from asking. She'd lost her mind inviting heartache like this.

"I am. Does that scare you? We haven't dated very long." He tapped her chin lightly as he resettled her in his arms, tugging the blanket up around her shoulders. "Funny how we've never really talked about all this."

That was part of a sentence. The rest of it was *until all this happened.* He had a point however, that they hadn't really opened up as to what they wanted this relationship to be.

"Not scared so much as surprised. Why me? There's nothing really special about me and, well, now you know that I have something of a checkered past. I'm not sure that makes me serious girlfriend material."

He lifted her chin so she had to look into his eyes. "Because you really see me and like me anyway."

"They didn't see…you?"

She could barely get the words out of her strangled throat. So much emotion had welled up as she'd gazed at him, his expression warm and loving.

"They saw what they wanted to see, never bothering to look any deeper or making me feel safe enough to show them all of who I am. I felt safe with you from that very first day."

"I'm glad," she said simply, not knowing what else to say. She was exhausted and her emotions were riding a roller coaster, which only succeeded in making her feel dizzy and nauseous. Her eyelids were beginning to feel heavy and she snuggled deeper into his arms, enjoying the heat of his body and the gentleness of his embrace.

"Sleep, angel. We can talk more in the morning. I think we're both tuckered out."

"I'm not that–" A yawn interrupted her protest and she gave in to the ever growing feeling of lethargy, the pills doing their job. She fell asleep with the steady thump of Travis's heart under her ear and the tender stroke of his fingers through her hair.

If only she could hold onto this paradise always.

Chapter Ten

SOME ASSHOLE WAS pounding on his hotel room door, completely disregarding the fact that Travis and Aubrey had managed only a few hours of sleep. After the events of the night before it was a miracle they'd slept as much as they had, honestly.

She had fallen asleep in his arms as they'd cuddled together on the chaise lounge on the patio and he'd carried her into her room and laid her on the bed. Not wanting to leave her alone, he'd joined her but slept on top of the covers so as not to alarm her if she woke unexpectedly. Right now she was frowning at the hammering on the door so he slid off the bed and strode through the living room, determined to punch whoever was making that infernal racket.

"This better fucking be important," he growled, yanking the door open and finding his cousin Shane on the other side, grinning like a lunatic. "You're here."

"Good morning to you too, Mister Obvious. Of course I'm here. You told me to come. So I grabbed the corporate jet and here I am. Does this joint have room service? Because I'm starved."

Shane strolled past Travis and tossed his duffle on the couch. His cousin was six years younger than Travis's forty-two but no one would ever miss the family resemblance. Shane had the same green eyes and dark hair although he wore his slightly longer.

"It's a five star resort so I would assume they have room service. Let me go see if Aubrey is awake and we can order some breakfast."

Travis didn't get far; the woman in question shuffling out of the bedroom wrapped in a hotel robe and yawning widely. Her hair was mussed and her eyes were sleepy. She was gorgeous. He'd never seen a woman look that good fresh out of bed, and his chest tightened with lust and some other emotion he didn't bother to name.

"Hungry, baby?"

He held out his arms and was gratified when she came into them willingly and without hesitation. He'd been actively working on that since they'd started dating, letting her know that his embrace was a safe place to be.

"A little. Mostly I have a nasty headache." Aubrey rubbed her temples but gave Shane a big hug and a smile. "Did you have a good flight? Did you get any sleep on the plane? We should order breakfast—you must be hungry."

Travis chuckled as Aubrey went into caretaker mode. She always did this with him or any of his family, and of course Shane was eating up all the attention with a spoon.

"The flight was fine and I did get some sleep. As for breakfast, I was just telling this ugly asshole that room service sounded pretty damn good. Omelets and hash browns for everybody."

"And bacon," Aubrey added perusing the menu. "Should I

just order a little of everything and we can share?"

"Order a lot of everything," Shane corrected, "and we'll share. I could eat a buffalo and still have room for dessert. Plus coffee. Lots of it. We have some work to do this morning."

That snagged Travis's attention. "Did Jason find anything?"

"He sent a text a few minutes ago that he's emailing you some information. He sounded tired. I think he and Jared have been up since you called him last night."

Travis wasn't going to feel guilty about that. Anything they could dig up that would take suspicion away from Aubrey was well worth the loss of sleep. He fired up his laptop and opened the email from Jason, perusing the attachments. His brother and colleagues had done a fine job for such short notice.

"Are you going to keep us in suspense?" Shane asked, trying to peer over Travis's shoulder. "Tell us what they found."

"I knew Bruce was an asshole but I had no idea about this. It's a powerful motivator for murder."

Aubrey was over his shoulder now as well. "What's the motive?"

Travis leaned back and gave her a smile. "Money, baby. Money."

They had a lead that didn't point in Aubrey's direction.

Things were looking up this morning.

✦ ✦ ✦

SHANE SHOVED ANOTHER forkful of hash browns into his mouth as the three of them sat around the dining table and ate breakfast. Aubrey had quickly showered and changed into a casual sundress and sandals before the food arrived. "So Bruce had a gambling problem? Who all did he owe money to?"

"Bookies, friends, and probably his wife and Martin. That wasn't his only vice. He liked fast women and booze as well. Your basic trifecta of sin," Travis answered with a shake of his head.

It appeared to Aubrey that Bruce Livingston hadn't changed much since high school.

Shane refilled his coffee and then Aubrey's as well. "Think he stole from Martin's firm? A guy like that wouldn't think twice about crossing a few lines of legality."

"He might have," Travis admitted. "Although Martin didn't say anything about money being missing. He only talked about insider trading. But now we know why Bruce might have been motivated to do that. If he owed that much money and was getting heat from his bookie then he might be pretty desperate."

"I don't feel sorry for him," Aubrey muttered, pushing her plate away. "I know that sounds terrible but he caused all his own problems. He was like this in school too. Everything was always someone else's fault. Another reason I stayed far away from him. I am sorry he's dead, though. No one deserves to be murdered."

"He sure as shit isn't the most sympathetic murder victim I've ever seen." Shane waved his fork in the air. "Honestly he sounds like a real douchebag. According to Jason this guy would have stolen candy from orphans. It's actually kind of surprising it took someone this long to kill him."

"Unfortunately they chose the weekend I was here. That cop thinks I did it."

Shane patted her hand. "I spent a few years in the public defender's office cutting my legal teeth in the beginning of my career, and I can tell you that cops are going to put you on the defensive when they question you. It's just a tactic and it doesn't mean that they think you're guilty. Hopefully this Prather guy is keeping an open mind. He'll need to with all the suspects he's going to have. Even if he arrests someone the prosecutor is going to have a bitch of a time with reasonable doubt. If they don't have some decent forensics this case will be a defense attorney's dream."

"A killer running loose," Aubrey groaned. "That doesn't make me feel any better, Shane."

"That would be scary if this were a random murder." Travis tapped the plate with his fingers. "But for now I think we need to go on the assumption that the killer chose Bruce for a compelling reason. Love. Money. Maybe revenge."

Shane hopped up from the table, coffee cup in hand, and began to pace back and forth. Whenever he was around he was like this, full of energy and life. The woman he ended up with was going to need a great deal of stamina to keep up with him. "So let's review. Who do we know that has a motive?"

"Me," she answered quietly. "He threatened to tell Travis a secret."

Shane nodded, but like the gentleman he was he didn't ask what she'd been keeping from his cousin. He was polite like that, as were all the Anderson men. If they didn't need to know something they didn't believe it was any of their business.

"But other than you," Shane pressed. "We should make a list."

Travis already had his laptop open since he had been conversing back and forth with Jason.

"I know Martin had a motive, as much as I hate to say it. Bruce's actions could bring down everything Martin has worked for and make him a pariah in the financial world."

"Plus his wife," Aubrey suggested. "If he was propositioning me I'm guessing I'm not the first. Plus Jason said he liked the ladies."

Travis tapped on the keyboard. "If you'd ever met Caroline you wouldn't think she was capable of hurting a fly, but you're right. To be thorough we have to include everyone on the list."

Shane paused and took a deep swig of his coffee. "The ones that don't seem like killers are the ones you have to be careful of. They're the most dangerous in my experience."

Does that include me? Or do I look like I could kill?

"His bookie. Basically anyone he owed money to," Travis offered. "I asked Jason to try and find out exactly who Bruce owed money to and how much. I also asked him to find out about Bruce's women. There might be a connection there."

Aubrey gestured to the laptop. "So we have a list. What now? Do we give it to Prather?"

Both Shane and Travis laughed and she had to slap the table hard to get their attention. She ought to be used to the almost spooky psychic connection these Anderson men had, but it never ceased to amaze her how their minds worked the same. She also wasn't all that fond of feeling like she didn't have a clue of what was going on.

"Baby, we're only going to help Prather if his investigation is going the wrong way. Even then it will just be a nudge here and there. I don't want anyone to think we're interfering in an official investigation. No, we'll start our own investigation and if we find something that Prather needs to know we'll give it to him. But right now I'm going on the assumption that he's not our friend."

Aubrey was sure that Prather wasn't any sort of friend. The only people she had on her side were Shane and Travis, but the two men were an awesome sight to behold. Without any doubt in her mind she knew they would do everything in their power to protect her from being falsely accused of Bruce's murder. But it couldn't all be up to them. She had to help herself and it was no time to be timid. They had a killer to hunt down.

"So where do we start?"

Chapter Eleven

M ARTIN'S WIFE ALANA opened the door of the suite and beckoned them to come in. Travis and Shane followed the woman out onto the large patio that overlooked the Gulf, the breeze soft and the sun warm overhead. Martin and his granddaughter Caroline were sitting at a large table that was laden down with food and drink. Apparently they weren't the first visitors that had stopped by this morning. Rising to his feet, Martin shook Travis's hand and ushered them into chairs.

"We came to pay our respects, my friend."

Travis and Shane accepted the glasses of iced tea from Alana and she urged them to fill a plate.

"The management sent up all this food. I'm guessing they want to keep all of this quiet," Alana said as she reached over to give her step-granddaughter Caroline a hug.

Bruce's now widowed wife always looked a little lost but today she appeared more frail than usual. Her long blonde hair was pulled back in a messy braid and her skin was pale and splotchy that contrasted with her red rimmed eyes. The last time he'd seen Bruce and Caroline together they hadn't been the picture of matrimonial happiness, but then the death of a spouse was likely to be a shock no matter the state of the relationship.

"We appreciate you stopping by." Caroline held out her hand to Travis and Shane. "It's been a long time since we saw you last."

"We're so sorry for your loss," Shane said smoothly, giving the young woman a gentle smile to help her feel at ease.

"Thank you. It's been a…shock."

Watching his friends through new eyes, Travis fucking hated what he was doing. There was no way Martin and his family had anything to do with Bruce's death but if he didn't talk to them, check them out then he wasn't doing a thorough job.

Aubrey needed nothing less than his absolute best. There would be no cut corners, no taking chances. She would be cleared completely and utterly before he was done.

"Do you have any idea who might have done this?" Travis sipped the iced tea and tried to keep his tone neutral. They didn't need to know he'd launched his own investigation.

"I can't imagine—" Caroline began but Alana cut her off mid-sentence.

"Stop trying to protect him, Caro. He's gone now and if his reputation is tarnished he has no one but himself to blame." Alana looked apologetically at Travis and Shane. "Bruce was not a very nice man, I'm afraid."

Caroline nodded in agreement, her voice shaky. "My husband is – excuse me – *was* a jerk. He treated me and everyone around him like they didn't matter. But he still didn't deserve to be stabbed to death, Alana."

Travis had suspected that Bruce had been knifed in the heart, but without a murder weapon he hadn't known for sure. Apparently Caroline had heard from the police on a possible cause of death.

"Bruce was a Class A bastard and everyone knew it."

Martin hadn't said much but his words hung in the air and no one seemed to want to contradict them in the least.

"You sure know how to bring a conversation to a complete halt," Travis chuckled, bringing some levity to the somber situation. "I'd like to hire you out for a business meeting I have coming up in a few weeks."

Martin smiled and ran his hand down his face with a long sigh. "I don't mean to be blunt, but the fact is Bruce had enemies."

Now they were getting somewhere. Travis needed to get Martin to open up even more as the older man had had Bruce investigated and probably knew a great deal about the deceased.

Travis helped himself to a pastry even though he'd already put away enough breakfast for a small family. "What kind of enemies?"

"The serious kind. The kind that don't fuck around." Martin looked at his wife and granddaughter apologetically. "Excuse my language, ladies. Bruce had problems and it made his life more dangerous than we could have ever understood. I told that to Detective Prather last night. Bruce owed money and I'm sure that's who killed him."

"He was making money in the markets. Why didn't he pay them off?" Travis asked, wanting to keep the conversation going in this direction. He'd known that Bruce had a bookie but perhaps Martin knew that person's name.

"It wasn't enough. He was spending money like water, faster

than he could make it. Thank God I nailed down Caro's trust fund so he couldn't get his dirty hands on it."

Caroline shifted in her chair uncomfortably. "He was still my husband and I don't think I want to stick around and listen to this. If you will excuse me?"

Alana stood along with Caroline and placed her arm around the trembling young woman. "It's the shock, Caro. You should take one of those pills the doctor prescribed for you in New York. It will help you get some rest. You need to keep your strength up."

Shaking her head, the young widow looked near tears. "I took one earlier. I hate how they make me feel. I'm not in control."

Alana led her step-granddaughter toward the large French doors to the suite. "Be a good girl and take one for me. I hate to see you this distraught. He wasn't worth it, sweetheart. He never was."

Caroline nodded meekly and allowed herself to be guided inside. A sedative explained the dull look in the girl's eyes and her general lethargic and depressed appearance.

With a sad expression Martin watched the two women disappear into the suite. "She hasn't loved Bruce for a long time but she feels guilty that she's relieved she's free."

"If he was that bad of a husband she has nothing to feel guilty about," Shane observed.

Martin let out a derisive snort. "He was that bad."

Shane was still staring at the doorway where the two women had exited. "Then I'm surprised she didn't leave."

"I think she was afraid. God only knows what Bruce threatened her with. At least now she can move on with her life." Martin leaned forward, his fingers steepled together. "If the offer to send her to the ranch is still open, Travis, I'd love to take you up on it. After the funeral, of course. This is going to be a circus and I want to protect her as much as possible from it."

"I'll help in any way I can," Travis assured his friend. "She's always welcome. You and Alana too, for that matter."

"We're fine. We can weather all the media bullshit. But Caroline has always been sort of fragile. I don't want her dragged through the mud by the newspapers. After everything she's been through she doesn't deserve that."

"I'll call Mom and Dad and make the arrangements. When and where is the service?"

"New York. We'll keep it as small and quiet as we can. As for when, I'm not sure. That detective doesn't want us leaving until he's sure that we're cleared." Martin grimaced as he took another sip of coffee. "I didn't like Bruce but I didn't kill him. That would have been too good for him. I wanted him behind bars being punished for what he's done."

Travis had to ask a delicate question, and it was probably best just to get it out rather than beat around the bush.

"Did you have a chance to talk to Bruce about the insider trading?"

Martin pushed his chair back from the table, a scowl crossing his face. "I did. He denied it all, of course. I told him he had the weekend to think about it, but on Monday if he didn't turn himself in then I was going to do it for him."

Travis rubbed his chin and quirked an eyebrow. "I can't imagine that went over well."

"It didn't," Martin agreed easily. "He stomped around and threw back a few whiskeys before heading back to the party. Last I saw him he was talking with Tom."

Tom Lovell had been a long-time friend and business partner of Bruce's, in addition to being a good friend to Martin. From what Travis had observed Tom was blind to Bruce's faults and had a bad case of hero worship.

"What time was that?"

Martin shrugged. "I don't know, maybe ten o'clock. You sound like that detective, Travis. Surely you don't think–"

"No way." Travis waved off the question before Martin could even ask it. "I've known you for years and I know that you wouldn't do something like this. I'm just trying to get an idea of the last few hours of Bruce's life. Who he talked to. What he did."

"Why? What interest do you have in all of this?"

Travis exchanged a glance with Shane before continuing. "The police questioned Aubrey last night. She and Bruce had an altercation that was witnessed by some of the party guests. He made a pass at her and she let him know his attentions were unwelcome."

"I wish I could say that I'm surprised but I'm not," Martin said dryly, refilling his coffee cup. "I hope your girl is all right. He didn't hurt her, did he?"

"She's fine but scared. That detective didn't go easy on her. I just want to make sure that he realizes there are more than enough suspects to go around and he doesn't have to concentrate on her."

"Bruce didn't have many friends. At least ones that weren't

with him for what he could buy. I still believe it was his bookie. Bruce owed them a lot of money."

"So what happens to all of his debts now? Will they come after you or worse, Caroline?"

His brows flying up in surprise, Martin was speechless for a moment. "I didn't even think about that. I just assumed if they killed him... Well, that this would all be over. You don't think they'd come after Caroline, do you?"

"They might," Shane conceded, sitting up straighter in his chair. "If they want the money owed to them, and they think you have it, they might contact you or your family. To my thinking, what you really need to be worried about is if they aren't the ones that murdered Bruce."

"Why is that? What makes that more worrisome?"

Shane didn't answer for a moment. "Because that may mean that Bruce was killed for a different reason, more personal reasons. And the more personal they are, the closer to home the killer is. If his bookie didn't do it then his friends or family did." Shane twirled the butter knife in his hand. "A knife is an up close and personal weapon, Martin. Whoever did this was someone who knew Bruce and knew him well. This wasn't a stranger murder. I guess what I'm trying to say is that you know the killer. They're someone close to you. That's just my guess."

Martin sat back in his chair, the blood drained from his face. "It can't be any of my friends and family. It can't be."

"I hope that's the case." Travis stood and walked to the railing to look out over the water. "But Shane has a point. If it's not his bookie, then who was Bruce closest to these last few years? Who did he spend the most time with?"

Martin's lips twisted in a pained smile. "That would be Iris. Iris Perry. His girlfriend. He flaunted his relationship with that woman for all to see."

"Is she in New York?"

Travis couldn't leave Aubrey here by herself to face Prather and she wasn't yet free to leave. But in the meantime, Iris could be booking a one way ticket to Rio, never to be seen again.

"She's right here in the resort," Martin replied bitterly. "Bruce didn't even have the decency to leave her at home for my birthday celebration."

Travis knew exactly who they needed to talk to next.

Chapter Twelve

"**G**EEZ, LITTLE SISTER, you go away for one weekend with tall, dark, and handsome and now you're wanted for a crime. You should never have left Montana. Should West and I fly out?"

Gigi's tone was filled with worry and Aubrey felt guilty that her sister had to take time out of planning her wedding to call during what was supposed to be a romantic weekend away.

A mini-vacation that had turned into a nightmare.

"No, you don't need to fly down here. I'm not actually wanted for a crime but I can't argue that it might have been smarter to stay in Montana," Aubrey agreed with a groan. "I knew this trip wouldn't be easy, what with all his wealthy friends, and don't forget the women that are constantly throwing themselves at him, but I never thought I'd actually see someone from my past."

Aubrey had reluctantly, and haltingly, told Gigi the entire story, including the promiscuous nature of her own behavior in high school.

"He sounds like a real dick." Gigi had a special way of summing things up. "And you have nothing to be ashamed of. It's okay for women to enjoy sex, you know. Hell, when West and I do it it's like time stops and the earth opens up or something. Anyway, it's fucking great. I bet Travis is as hot between the sheets as West is. There's something about these Anderson men."

As much as Aubrey loved her sister and thought West was a terrific guy, she could do without the sexual details of their intimate lives. Aubrey had very carefully not said a whole lot about her own, but something inside was pressing her to confide in someone who cared.

"I wouldn't know."

There. She'd said it.

"What? What wouldn't you know?" Gigi sounded confused and Aubrey didn't blame her.

"I wouldn't know if Travis is hot between the sheets. We…we haven't slept together. Yet, I mean."

The silence almost went on so long Aubrey thought the line on her cell phone had dropped.

"You haven't slept with Travis?" Gigi sucked in a breath. "Honey, he's hotter than a firecracker in July. What are you waiting for?"

Courage.

"I–I just haven't yet. I didn't want to rush into it."

Wow, that sounded stupid. Even Aubrey didn't believe a word that was coming out of her mouth.

"Oh. Well, that's okay. I probably should have waited longer with West but I just couldn't help myself. You're a stronger woman than I am." Neither sister said a word. "You are attracted to Travis, aren't you, sis? I mean…does he treat you okay?"

Aubrey had been pacing the floor of her bedroom but now

she fell back against the bed pillows with a noisy sigh. "He treats me like a princess, and yes, he's sexy. And gorgeous. It's just that…"

Saying it out loud made it more real, although she'd been living it so it didn't get much more real than that.

"Just what?" Gigi prompted. "You know you can tell me anything, right? Did someone hurt you, sis?"

"No one hurt me." Aubrey rubbed her temples, a headache beginning to bloom after all the crap that had happened in the last twenty-four hours. "It's just that I haven't had sex since I was seventeen and I'm nervous."

That last sentence had rushed out at lightning speed, the words running together. Luckily Gigi didn't need anything repeated.

"Seventeen? Holy crap on a cracker, girl, seventeen? Why? I mean, well, yeah—let's start there. Why? Not that there's anything wrong with it. I mean, I can respect your choices and everything. Aww shit, I've messed this up, haven't I? What I'm trying to say is that it's okay if you're not into it. You don't have to be and you don't owe anyone any explanations. I support you in whatever you choose."

Aubrey rested her head in her hand, humiliation turning her cheeks hot despite her sister being a thousand miles away and unable to see her. "Thank you. I appreciate that. I'm not sure I really chose this route or it chose me. It's hard to explain. Honestly I'm not sure I can."

But Gigi simply waited patiently, not saying a word, letting Aubrey gather her scattered and very embarrassed thoughts until she had an idea of how to describe all the conflicting emotions inside.

"I'm very attracted to Travis and I do want to go to bed with him."

It was the understatement of the century. She was dying to sleep with him.

"You don't have to. I know I may have sounded like I was pushing you but I swear I'm not. I don't want you to feel pressured to do something you don't want to do."

"I'm pushing myself much more than you ever could," Aubrey admitted quietly. "I want to be with him. I actually crave being close to him, Gigi. I love being in his arms. I love the way he smells and the warmth of his skin. I literally get weak in the knees when he kisses me."

"I think that's wonderful that you feel this way but I'm sure Travis is okay with waiting if that's what you need."

"He is. He's been really patient. I just...dammit, I'm just terrified."

Admitting it didn't make her feel any better, sadly. It only made her fear more three-dimensional as her intestines seemed to twist into a painful knot and sweat began to pool on the back of her neck. The mere thought of making love with Travis turned her into a mess of nerves.

"What are you afraid of? Pregnancy?" Gigi's voice had dropped to a whisper as if she was afraid someone was listening on the line. "Are you on the pill or something? I can recommend a doctor if you aren't."

Running her damp palms on the fabric of her sundress, Aubrey took a deep calming breath. "I'm not afraid of an unplanned pregnancy, although as I told you that's what stopped my self-destructive behavior in high school. My friend Debbie got pregnant and had to drop out. No, I'm on the pill and I have no reason to believe it wouldn't work."

"That's good. So when it feels right, you're ready. There's no reason to push yourself into it, sis. You'll know when it's right. Until then, relax and just enjoy being courted and wooed. These Anderson men really know how to romance a girl."

"I think there's something wrong with me."

She'd said it out loud.

"Can you be slightly more specific?"

"I–I really don't enjoy it." The words choked in her throat. "At all. I'm not sure what all the fuss is about."

"Is that what all this drama is about? Aubrey, I'm not surprised. You had sex with groping, teenage boys. Men – good men, anyway – do things much differently. They actually care if you're having a good time."

"I don't want to disappoint Travis. What if the problem is me?"

She was well aware she was trying Gigi's patience. Logically Aubrey knew what Gigi said made sense, but this situation had very little to do with logic and everything to do with emotion.

"What if it isn't? Trust me, there are a bunch of really selfish assholes out there who have no clue about the female anatomy. And don't care to learn. Just answer me this…do you enjoy it when Travis kisses you?"

Oh hell yes.

"Of course I do."

"Does the room get warm and your heart race?"

"How did you know that? Are you some sort of creepy Peeping Tom on my dates with Travis? Do I need to have a talk with West about you walking in your sleep perhaps?"

Gigi's giggles filled Aubrey's ear. "I know because that's how I feel with West, and I can tell you from experience that if you feel that way it is not you. I've had some pretty crappy sex too. With the right guy? It's great. The only thing you have to ask yourself is if Travis is the right man. Don't let me, Travis, society, or anyone else push you into anything. It's okay if you don't want to have sex. It's okay if you do but you want to wait. For later. For marriage. Whatever. It's okay, sis."

The only place pressure was coming from was from herself. She'd put herself in this predicament and only she could stop it.

"I want to. You know, when the time is right."

"There you go. It will happen when it happens. In the meantime cut yourself some slack. Don't have sex with him because you think you should or because you're grateful that he didn't think you were a slut. Neither one of those reasons are good ones. You'll only regret it afterward and I think you already have enough sex issues without adding to them, don't you think?"

Too many and it was time to do something about them.

"I want it to be right. I know that sounds childish."

"You've closed off a very important part of yourself for a long time, sis, and it's only natural that you want your return to it to be something special. It should be. If it's not, then don't do it."

"You make sense. I'm putting a lot of pressure on myself for everything to be perfect."

Aubrey heard Gigi's sharp intake of breath. "Ohhhh, I get it now. You want it to be the deflowering you didn't get in high school."

Rolling over to her stomach, Aubrey buried her face in a pillow. "It's so stupid. I've heard other women's stories and I know it's not puppies and unicorns most of the time, so I'm not sure why I'm so obsessed with making the first time with Travis so wonderful."

"I'll easily admit my first time was nothing to write home about." Gigi laughed on the other end of the line. "The only thing positive I can really say is that it was over quickly, which was probably a blessing because it hurt like a bitch."

Aubrey remembered her own first time vividly. "I wish my first time was for a better reason than wanting love and attention from some jerk."

"Do you think my first time was much better?" Gigi scoffed. "Hell, I was pressured into it by my boyfriend who said that if I really loved him I'd put my mouth on his dick. It certainly wasn't because I couldn't help myself like with West."

"I wished I'd waited until Travis. If I had then I wouldn't be going through all this nonsense."

More laughter. Aubrey was glad she could amuse Gigi with all her problems. "If you had waited then you'd be nervous about the unknown. Face it, sis. We're damned if we do and damned if we don't. If we have sex and enjoy it, we're sluts. If we don't have sex or enjoy it, then we're repressed and something is wrong with us. We should just do whatever the hell we want and forget about everyone else."

Gigi was absolutely right. Aubrey had been letting herself worry about other people for far too long. "Did I mention that you're the best big sister ever?"

"I'm always here for you, no matter what."

"As much as I love Zach this probably isn't something he could have helped me with," Aubrey sighed, thinking about her

OLIVIA JAYMES

adorable brother. He wasn't a virgin by any means but he liked to pretend that she and Gigi were.

"If Zach could he'd put chastity belts on the two of us and castrate West and Travis. All of this definitely stays between us. Are you going to be okay now? I was serious about West and I flying down there if you need us."

Big sister would save little sister at the drop of a hat, but Aubrey had been on her own for too long to allow that to happen.

"I'm fine. Travis is here and so is Shane. I'm as safe as a kitten."

"I'm not sure any woman has used the words 'safe' and 'Shane' in the same sentence, but if you're sure…"

The sound of Travis and Shane at the suite door made Aubrey hop off the bed. "They're back. I want to hear what they learned from Martin. Can I call you later?"

"You better. Keep me in the loop."

Aubrey rang off and stepped into the living room where the two men were already sitting on the couch, deep in conversation.

"What happened? What did he say?"

Travis tugged her down next to him and pressed a soft kiss on her temple. "I have a favor to ask you, baby."

She'd climb Mount Everest for this man.

"Name it."

"I'd like to treat you to a luxury day at the spa. All the trimmings. Manicure, pedicure, facial, massage, plus anything else we can find. What do you say?"

From the sly expression on his face this wasn't just about treating her like a princess, but who was she to turn down a day of pampering?

"I'm in. Now tell me why I'm really doing this."

Chapter Thirteen

"**H**AVE A SEAT and Mary will be right with you."

Aubrey climbed into the pedicure chair, careful not to spill the glass of Chablis the spa staff had poured for her. Wrapped in a fluffy white robe and slippers, she'd spent most of the day being massaged and beautified. The only item left was a mani-pedi.

It was her last chance to meet up with Iris Perry, Bruce's girlfriend. Shane had done some snooping around this morning after she refused to talk to them about Bruce. Iris was spending the day in the spa which was the motivator behind Travis sending Aubrey here for the full treatment. She'd been exfoliated, plucked, and massaged to within an inch of her life but she hadn't been able to maneuver anywhere near Bruce's girlfriend. Now Aubrey was finally sitting next to Iris for at least the next thirty minutes if not more, and the woman couldn't get up and walk away with wet toe polish.

Aubrey relaxed back in the heated chair and sighed, a contented smile on her lips. "I could get used to this."

The woman next to her smiled as well, lifting her wine glass in a toast. "No kidding. This is exactly what I needed today."

Iris Perry was an attractive woman in her mid to late twenties with copper colored hair and dark eyes. She was also draped in a thick white robe but Aubrey could easily see that the woman sported a neat, trim figure. Not surprising.

Bruce had never spent much time or energy on unattractive females.

"Rough week?" Aubrey asked innocently. "My boss has been running me ragged but my boyfriend treated me to a day of pampering. He's the best."

Shane and Travis had coached Aubrey unmercifully about this conversation and being careful in general, but Iris had given her an opportunity to bring up boyfriends right off the bat.

"You're lucky. Most men are too cheap. They only do things that have some benefit to themselves."

The spa manager refilled Iris's empty wine glass. Hopefully the alcohol would loosen her tongue.

"Sounds like you need a new man. What's your type?"

Iris took a big drink and laughed, her hand over her mouth as if she didn't want to tell a secret.

"The same type any girl wants. Handsome. Built. Rich. Generous. Your typical Prince Charming. Is that too much to ask?" The woman sighed, her gaze fixed somewhere in the distance. "Men like that don't grow on trees. I've maybe met one man who fit that description. What about you?"

Keep it light but keep her talking.

"My boyfriend is pretty wonderful, and sexy as hell. But he's not perfect, of course. I think every man has at least a few good qualities. I'm sure your boyfriend has a couple."

"He loves me and that's what's important. He's also gorgeous."

Aubrey had to fight the urge to frown or laugh. Iris must not have that high of a standard. "He sounds pretty great. How long have you been together?"

"About a year, give or take. What about you?"

The wine was doing its thing. Iris's face was flushed and her eyes were glazed over. The staff had been plying them with booze all day long, although Aubrey had kept her intake to a minimum.

"A month. Not long, really. We're in the new stage I guess you would call it."

Iris giggled and tossed back the rest of her wine. "I love the beginning. It's all sex and puppy dog eyes."

"You need more wine." Aubrey pointed to Iris's glass. "I'll get someone's attention."

"I shouldn't have any more. I'll be asleep before dinner at this rate."

"You look like a woman that can handle her drink."

Aubrey wasn't above flattering Iris if it would help. So far the entire conversation was quite surreal. Iris was speaking about Bruce as if he were still alive. The praise she'd heaped upon the deceased also seemed strange since he had few friends to compliment him.

"Maybe one more," Iris agreed with a sleepy smile. "I really needed this today. It's been a bitch of a weekend so far."

"That's terrible. What happened?" Aubrey asked casually. "Work troubles?"

"Just too much going on."

Really? Her boyfriend being murdered didn't even make the

list? What the hell?

"I guess it could have been worse. I heard someone died at a party here in the hotel last night." Aubrey shuddered and took another sip of her wine. "It made me want to pack my things and check out right away."

There was a telling moment of silence and Iris's features had turned bland, completely devoid of any sort of strong emotion. "I doubt there is a killer running loose that's going from room to room murdering guests of the hotel. I think I saw something on a television show once about the odds of being murdered. They weren't high."

Iris didn't look worried. Interesting.

"It's still creepy. I can't wait to get out of here."

Aubrey hoped to turn the conversation toward the details of the crime to see if Iris might inadvertently let something slip, but she didn't have a chance. A sunny eighties tune began to play and Iris reached into her robe pocket and pulled out her phone.

"Excuse me. I have a call."

Frustrated, Aubrey waited but the woman chatted for the next several minutes, mostly just answering "yes" and "no" but never saying anything that would reveal who she was speaking to and what they were talking about. Iris was still on the phone when her pedicure was complete and she was exiting the salon. Aubrey gave her a wave and Iris nodded absently in return, still engrossed in her call.

Who was she talking to so intently?

It didn't look like Aubrey was going to find out. She'd learned very little today but one thing was very clear.

Iris Perry wasn't mourning the loss of Bruce. Not one little bit.

✦   ✦   ✦

"THAT'S STRANGE." TRAVIS perused the menu while the waiter scuttled away to fill their bar order. "She didn't say anything at all about Bruce's death. Not a word?"

After Aubrey's day of beauty, Travis had insisted on them dressing up and going out to dinner at a classy French restaurant just a few blocks from the resort. She'd chosen a flame red cocktail dress with thin spaghetti straps and he was in a gorgeous heather gray suit that looked like it was made for him.

Damn hot.

She was so aroused by his "suit porn" her knees were jelly and her hands were trembling. Her mind might be hesitating to make love to him but her body was all systems go.

"Not a word. She acted like he was still alive, which was really kind of creepy. She also said he was gorgeous." Aubrey made a face of distaste. She didn't feel good about speaking ill of the dead but Bruce hadn't done much to endear himself to her. Or anyone, for that matter. "Ick. She must really love him if she feels that way."

"But then wouldn't she be upset? Sad? You didn't describe a woman torn up with grief."

"She was drinking an awful lot. Maybe that's how she processes death. And talking about him like he's still alive? She could be deeply in denial."

"She could be guilty as hell too," Travis retorted with a grin as their drinks were placed in front of them. Jameson on the rocks for him and a cranberry and vodka for her.

"What was her motive? If they were happy there would be no reason to kill him."

Travis closed his menu and placed it on the edge of the table. "I don't know what her motive would be. Maybe money? According to Martin she was holding all of Bruce's ill-gotten gains from his insider trading. She might not have wanted to split it with him."

The waiter interrupted them and Aubrey ordered the coq au vin and Travis ordered the beef bourguignon, followed by a chocolate soufflé with a Chantilly crème that they would share.

"So Iris didn't give us anything but more confusion. Where do we go from here?"

Travis reached across the table and captured her hand, lifting it so his lips could brush the knuckles. A shiver ran up her spine and that familiar ache between her thighs began to make itself known.

"I'm glad you asked that. Jason is digging into Bruce's financial affairs and found out that he owes Tom Lovell almost two hundred thousand dollars from a joint real estate deal gone bad. Apparently they invested in some property that was going to skyrocket in value but that didn't happen. Then Tom found out he'd overpaid for the land in the first place and the person they bought it from was a good friend of Bruce's. See where this is going?"

"Business is cutthroat, isn't it?"

She'd seen Travis in meetings and dinners, more than she could count, and it had never ceased to amaze her how downright nasty people could be to one another. It all looked civilized on the surface but underneath it was a street fight to the death.

"It is, baby. Dog eat dog, and all that. Apparently Tom threatened to sue so Bruce signed a promissory note to pay the money back, but he hadn't so far. Maybe Tom got tired of waiting."

"Let me guess. Tom is here this weekend?"

The rich and famous were certainly different. In Aubrey's experience, people who owed each other money didn't hang out together and act like friends. In fact, they usually avoided being in the same room.

"He is. I think we should pay him a visit tomorrow and see what he has to say."

"I hope we have more luck than I did today. Do you know him very well?"

"Pretty well. From what I've seen he's a nice guy who may not be the greatest businessman or judge of character. According to Jason, Tom is clean and doesn't have any unusual or expensive vices unless you count a string of polo ponies."

Aubrey sipped her drink, the cranberry tart on her tongue. "He plays polo. Now that's a sport that they don't show on television very often. Do you play?"

Travis laughed, that dimple flashing in his cheek. "Are you kidding? I ride broncos, honey, not polo ponies. You want a trust fund baby I can introduce you to several this weekend, but that's not me."

Images of Travis in his well-fitting old blue jeans, worn boots, and a flannel shirt were making Aubrey uncomfortably warm. She'd seen him tame a wild horse and it had been incredibly erotic to watch how gentle and sweet, yet firm, he was with the animal. Completely in control and totally trustworthy. The horse had ended up eating a sugar cube out of Travis's palm.

"I don't think that's really my type." She gave him a flirtatious look from under her lashes. "I already have my eye on someone."

Travis growled but his eyes lit up playfully. "Tell me his name. I want to know my competition."

Aubrey giggled, pretending to hesitate. "I don't know if I should say it. I wouldn't want to start anything."

"I bet he's a loser."

Shaking her head, she leaned forward so only he could hear her. "Far from it. He's handsome and sweet. Smart and successful." Something inside made her bold. "And I adore him. When he kisses me my knees go weak."

Clearly she'd lost her damn mind. What on earth made her say that out loud? Her momentary courage had flown the coop and now she had to press her hand to her stomach so she wouldn't throw up. She didn't want him to think she was pushy. She didn't want to give him the chance to reject her.

But Travis didn't think she'd gone too far. Their gazes locked and he was looking at her like she was a juicy T-bone and he was a hungry lion.

Oh shit.

"Then there's no chance for me?" His smile grew wider and her heart skipped a few beats. "It sounds like you might be in love with him."

Love? Did he use that four-letter word?

She wasn't ready to say it. She wasn't even sure she was ready to feel it.

Did he love her?

Aubrey was so nervous she thought she might faint. Her pulse fluttered and she had to concentrate to keep her breathing even.

Apparently Travis didn't expect her to respond, which was good because her mouth and tongue didn't seem to be working properly. Instead he smoothly changed the subject to the mine contract they'd sewed up right before this weekend and what it would mean when they returned to the office in a few days.

Her heart rate returned to almost normal and she didn't feel like tossing her cookies any more.

A temporary reprieve only. Travis was still looking at her with an almost feral intensity. When they returned to the suite things were bound to get interesting.

Would they or wouldn't they?

She didn't know the answer but her body was begging for a definite yes.

It was wrestling her stubborn brain to the ground and giving it a wedgie.

It was going to be a cage match to the death. Winner take all.

Chapter Fourteen

TRAVIS HAD PUSHED too hard at dinner.

He'd mentioned love and it was way too soon, really. But, dammit, he wasn't some callow youth who didn't know what he wanted in a woman. He was a grown ass man, over forty, who had been around the block more times than he could count or remember. Finding a wonderful woman like Aubrey felt like a miracle after all these years. He'd given up hope of there being a woman out there who cared about him for himself and not the Anderson fortune. If he lost everything tomorrow she'd still be by his side, of that he had no doubt.

"Do you want to watch some television?" Travis asked as they entered the suite. They needed a distraction from the tension brewing between them, and Aubrey had mentioned she was too keyed up to sleep. "We could order in a movie or something."

She kicked off her high heels with a relieved sigh. "That sounds like a great idea. Let me get changed and take off my makeup."

Aubrey slipped into her room and Travis quickly shrugged out of his suit, replacing it with a pair of sweat pants and a t-shirt. He padded out to the living room and picked up the television guide on the coffee table to see what movies were playing. There was a romantic comedy she would enjoy and the latest blockbuster superhero flick as well.

"Did you pick one out?"

Wearing pink cotton pajama pants and a matching tank top, Aubrey looked impossibly young. Her face was scrubbed of any cosmetic artifice and her feet were bare with cherry red tipped toes from her pedicure earlier in the day.

A wave of unaccustomed insecurity washed over him as he gazed at this tiny woman who had the power to hurt him so much. She was young, not yet thirty, and he was over forty. He worried that eventually she'd grow bored with him or worse, that he wouldn't be able to satisfy her. At his age he couldn't make love all night anymore, although he was no slouch in that department. Just because he couldn't come a dozen times a night didn't mean she couldn't. He'd be more than happy to make sure she experienced multiple orgasms every single day of her life if she wanted them.

"I'm not fussy. What do you think?"

He held out the guide and she pointed to the superhero movie with a delighted smile. "This one. I love these, especially the bad guys. Is that all right?"

He far preferred it over the romance, but he would never have said no if she chose the other one.

"That was my choice too. Let's get comfy on the sofa."

This had to be the best part of Travis's day. Any day. He worked his tail off from morning to night, but then he was able to snuggle up to the most beautiful woman in the world for a few hours and pretend the rest of the world didn't exist. Perfection.

He was lying behind her so that she was between his legs, her back resting on his chest. He wrapped his arms around her waist and stroked an exposed patch of skin right above her hip while his chin rested on the top of her head. Time seemed to come to a standstill as they watched the movie, their limbs entwined. He could smell the vanilla of her shampoo and feel the steady beat of her heart. The rise and fall of her chest with each breath was subtly hypnotic and he had to struggle to stay focused and not be swept away with all the delicious sensations she evoked just being this close. He was certain she could feel him half hard against the curve of her spine.

"Are you hungry? Or thirsty? Can I get you something?"

Travis really didn't want to disturb their peace but manners had been hammered into him from a young age. Even when all he wanted to do was lift her into his arms and carry her to his bedroom.

Aubrey twisted in his arms so she was facing him. "I'm fine. Do you not like the movie? We can watch something else if you'd rather."

Actually I'd like to throw you over my shoulder and carry you to my bed where I'll ravish you like there's no tomorrow.

"This movie is fine," he said, instead of what he really wanted to. "I just wanted to make sure you were okay."

Tilting her head, she gazed at him for a long moment. "I'm okay. But you seem like you're in a strange mood. You have been all evening. Is it this whole Bruce thing? You've gone beyond the call of duty and I'm more than grateful, but I'll understand if you want to bail on all this. You can go back to Tremont in the morning and I can stay here until the cops let me leave. I'll come back as soon as they do."

"Shit. No." He'd fucked this up and needed to fix it fast. "That's not it at all. I'm not leaving you here by yourself. It's just—"

He broke off, more unsure of her than any woman he'd ever dated and that included every girlfriend he'd had as a teenager. Aubrey made him feel like a pimply, geeky kid again.

"Just what?" she prompted softly. "Have I done something, Travis? I'm sorry if I have."

She was apologizing and he was the horny lecherous asshole here.

"You haven't done anything wrong. This is all me, kitten. I'm the problem."

Dear God, he hoped she'd simply drop the entire thing but he couldn't be that lucky.

"Then what's going on? You haven't been yourself. If it's not Bruce and it's not me…is it Martin? Are you worried about him? Or is it something at the office? Maybe I can help."

Christ, her gentle questioning, worrying about his well-being, was going to be the undoing of him.

"Baby, maybe it's time for us to turn in. We have a big day tomorrow. We need to talk to Tom and then find out where Prather is in his investigation."

Without Prather realizing what they were doing, of course.

Her expression turned to one of hurt and she nodded without a word, climbing off of the couch and leaving him aroused and frustrated. She had no idea why he was and clearly she thought it was her fault. His sexual frustration with the status quo was his own impatience.

"Sure. Okay. I'll guess I'll see you in the morning."

Head hanging, Aubrey walked toward her bedroom door and the pressure in Travis's gut suddenly seemed too much to bear.

"I want you, okay?" Shit, he needed to shut the hell up. The words had come out desperate, which he had never in his life been until this woman. "I'll wait forever for you, sweetheart, but you need to know that sometimes it's not easy and tonight is one of those times."

Aubrey whirled around and her mouth had fallen open in surprise, a blush staining her cheeks. Her cute little chin lifted and she walked back to him, placing her hands on his chest.

"I don't want to wait anymore."

And just that fast he was harder than a fence post.

"Baby, we don't have to rush into anything. I can wait. Hell, it's probably good for me. It'll build character or something."

He tried to give her a gentle, reassuring smile while at the same time he fought his caveman instincts to throw her on the bed and take her now.

"I don't want to wait." She paused as if she wasn't sure how to convince him but he was more than willing to be persuaded. "I want you."

Yes, ma'am. He was all hers.

✦ ✦ ✦

AUBREY THOUGHT TRAVIS might rip her clothes off or throw her over his shoulder fireman style, but he did neither. Despite the wild look in his eye he carefully and slowly leaned down to capture her lips with his own. Her mouth blossomed under his as his tongue sought entry. He explored, tickled, and rubbed the cavern of her mouth until she was breathless and her panties damp.

"Travis," she breathed, trying to catch her breath. "Take me."

"I intend to do just that. I'm going to make you mine until you can't remember a time before we made love, before I was deep inside you."

A rush of moisture flooded her panties and her heart thumped painfully against her ribcage. The deep, dark timbre of his voice promised all manner of pleasure and any doubts that remained in her troublesome brain were shushed into silence. Tonight was about reclaiming what she'd lost so long ago. With the man she adored. The man she trusted more than anyone.

He reached down and swept her up into his arms and carried her into the bedroom, his gaze never straying from her own. Setting her gently down on the bed, he crawled up her body until he was hovering above her own, his wide shoulders blocking out the rest of the room.

"I've wanted you from the first moment I laid eyes on you," he growled, leaning down to brush butterfly kisses across her lips, forehead, cheekbones, and finally the hollow below her ear. "Tell me what you want. Tell me what you fantasize about and I'll make it come true. I want to give you everything you've ever wanted."

Mouth hanging open, Aubrey had no idea what to say. She'd never expected anyone to ask the question. "I–I'm not sure. I don't know."

"Do you like it hard and fast or soft and slow? Do you want

me to say dirty things in your ear? Do you like to come right away or do you like to wait until you can't hold back anymore?"

Holy Mary, Mother of God. It all sounded good. Every bit of it. There was no way she could choose.

"Yes." The word came out as a whisper so she said it again. "Yes."

His brow knitted but then he smiled. "All of it? I guess we have all night. Just so you know I like a little dirty talk in my ear as well. If you're taking suggestions."

Was she? She'd spoken rarely during sex and usually only answered direct questions. She wasn't sure she could keep up some filthy dialogue about an act she hadn't done in years. She really didn't have a clue as to what she was doing and she doubted she could fool him. He had too much experience.

His fingers tangled in her hair and his lips trailed over her jaw and down her neck to where her pulse beat frantically under her skin. He nipped at the sensitive flesh before soothing it with his tongue, and a frantic moan of pleasure escaped from her lips. A rush of arousal ran through her and her body shook with its pure power. She'd never wanted anyone as much as she wanted Travis.

Skilled hands slid under her tank top, leaving a trail of fire everywhere they touched. She expected him to pull it over her head and toss it away but he froze, a frown taking the place of the smile that had been there only moments before.

"Kitten? Are you okay? Do you want me to stop?"

Aubrey didn't know why he was asking at first, but then she felt the pads of his fingers tenderly brush her cheeks before holding them up for her inspection.

Wet.

She was crying and she'd had no idea.

So overwhelmed with emotions and sensation, she'd handled it the only way she knew how. Now he was going to think she was a blubbering mess. She had to explain or he was going to think she'd lost what was left of her sanity.

"I'm okay. I don't want to stop."

"You're crying," he whispered, his expression bordering on tortured. It was her fault he felt this way. "Am I hurting you?"

She swallowed the lump that had taken up residence in her throat and shook her head. "It's just been a long time for me and I guess all the emotions became too much. But it's all good. Really."

Travis sat back on his haunches, still not looking convinced. "When you say a long time, what does that mean exactly?"

Her fingers worried at the silky sheets, hoping she could find an elegant way to verbalize her pathetic situation.

"It means...it means that I haven't had sex in a very long time. Like...years."

"Years," he repeated carefully. "How many years are we talking about here? A couple?"

Licking her suddenly dry lips, she screwed up her courage one more time. "Almost ten years. Since I was seventeen." His eyes widened at her confession. "I just haven't met anyone that I really wanted until now. And well...honestly, I didn't think I was missing much anyway. If you must know, I don't think I'm very good at this."

He knew everything now. She only hoped he wouldn't turn and leave.

Chapter Fifteen

N*INE YEARS.*

Aubrey hadn't had sex in nine years.

Travis kept repeating the words inside his head but he was having trouble truly understanding their meaning. The warm armful of woman currently lying on his bed and underneath him was the sexiest female he'd ever seen. There was no way in hell she'd kept what had to be droves of horny males at arm's length for that long.

It was impossible.

Yet she was looking up at him with the most earnest expression. She appeared to be serious.

If she was…why?

Why deny herself the pleasure of lovemaking? It didn't make any sense.

Was she punishing herself for what she considered poor behavior when she was in high school?

He ran her words through his befuddled mind one more time and finally came up with a possibility, remembering what she'd said when she'd told him about her past.

"Why do you think you're no good at this?"

Aubrey squirmed as if trying to slide away, but he placed his hands on either side of her head so he could look into her eyes.

"I've never...you know...with a man. Ever. So I figure it must be me. Even though Gigi says it's not."

It took him a moment but realization flashed and he leaned forward so they were almost nose to nose.

"I can guarantee you, baby, that it isn't you." He all but growled the words, anger at the selfish boys she'd been with that had taken what they wanted without giving anything in return. "You had sex with boys. I've left those years long behind. Things are going to go a hell of a lot different here tonight. Trust me when I say that you *can* and you *will feel pleasure*. I won't stop until you *do*. More than once. That's a promise."

Pink suffused her skin from her chest to her turned-up nose. "I'm nervous. Really, really nervous. Honest to God, I think I might pass out kind of nervous."

Her sweet uncensored confession made his heart constrict so tightly it hurt to take a breath.

"I have an idea. Why don't you just lie back and relax and let me take the reins. When, or if, you feel comfortable then you can touch and kiss me, but until then this show is all about you. How does that sound?"

"Like an impossible dream."

Clearly his Aubrey didn't think she was capable of great passion, but he'd already seen the signs in her long ago when he'd kissed her for the first time. Her body had responded immediately, no hesitation, pure and honest. She didn't play the games he'd been subjected to by the women who were looking to "land a rich husband". She wanted what he was and he wanted every bit of her.

Reaching under her tank top he slowly lifted it, giving her ample time to stop him if she wanted to. He tossed it to the floor, revealing round, firm breasts with petal pink nipples that begged for his fingers and tongue. He had to steel himself not to fall on her like a starving dog on a bone. Instead he hooked his thumbs in the waistband of her pajama pants, gliding them down her legs until all that covered her gorgeous body was a lacy strip of pink panties that were doing dangerous things to his blood pressure.

He could hear his heartbeat roaring in his ears as he pressed his lips to her quivering abdomen. Her skin was soft, silky, and warm to the touch and he trailed wet kisses from her belly button, up through the valley between her breasts, and then back down until his tongue ran along the edge of her panties. Her body trembled under his touch, leaving him in no doubt she was as affected as he was by what was taking place between the two of them.

His hands slid up her torso, cupping her generous breasts in his palms and teasing the already hard nipples with this thumbs. His groin tightened painfully, tenting the soft material of his sweatpants, reminding him that he had to control his arousal or this evening would come to a much earlier conclusion than he wanted. He hoped that at his age he'd managed to garner a little more control than when he was an impatient youth, but at the moment he felt about eighteen.

"Do you like this, kitten? Do you want more?"

Aubrey moved restlessly under him, her body pressing closer to his own as he leaned down to capture a straining nipple into his mouth, lapping at the hard tip before scraping it gently with his teeth. Her body arching, her fingers slid into his hair and dug into his scalp, the nails erotically scratching the skin.

He switched his attention to her other breast, then back and forth until she was mewling with pleasure under his eager attentions. Sliding his mouth in a southerly direction, he swirled his tongue at the sensitive juncture where hip met thigh, drawing a breathy moan from her lips before tugging the final silky barrier down her tanned legs. He tossed them onto the pile of clothes on the floor and pressed kisses to her inner thigh, nipping a path to her wet and waiting slit.

He lowered his mouth to her, anticipation building in his lower back and balls. She sent his senses into overdrive, her scent, her taste, her feel, the way she moaned as his tongue teased her, and the way she arched her back up off of the mattress in sheer unadulterated ecstasy.

He pursed his lips around her clit and gently sucked, and she responded with a half-scream, her thighs pressing on each side of his face. He braced his hands against them, forcing them apart again as he rolled his tongue in a circle around the sensitive bundle of nerves.

"Travis..." she whimpered, her fingers scrambling for purchase on his shoulders, her body bowed with pleasure. He refused to give her respite, savoring every second of her impending climax as he pushed two fingers into her, curling them to stroke at the sweet spot deep inside.

She was close. Very soon she'd know that there wasn't a thing in this world she'd done wrong.

✦   ✦   ✦

TRAVIS HADN'T LIED when he'd promised her she'd find heaven in his arms tonight. But this heaven wasn't soft and peaceful. No, this involved sweaty bodies, tongues, fingers, and thighs sticky with her own honey. She writhed and moaned as her orgasm built relentlessly, painful in its intensity. It was like nothing she'd ever experienced in her life and she wanted it to go on and on forever, and yet at the same time she wanted to let it shatter her into a million pieces so she could start all over again.

Finally the pressure coiled in her abdomen was too much and it sprang free as her breath stuttered out of her lungs and her body shook with the force of her release. Her lids fluttered shut and colored lights danced in front of her eyes as the universe swirled until she was dizzy and out of breath.

Aubrey dragged air into her starved lungs as Travis placed a tender kiss on her hip and sat back on his heels again, sliding his sweatpants down his legs and tossing them to the floor. His t-shirt was the next to go, revealing his tanned, muscular chest. Feeling particularly bold she reached up and ran her hands over the smooth flesh, tracing his ridged abs and tickling his hip-bones, eliciting a low groan that seemed pulled from the depths of his soul. Her fingers brushed the tented fabric of his boxers and he threw back his head and moaned, giving her the courage to explore him more fully.

Impatiently he tugged at his boxers, throwing them on the floor, his length springing free and slapping his belly. Long and hard, he was larger than anything she'd seen before and she knew a moment of fear that she couldn't take him. He seemed to recognize her reticence and he wrapped his hand around the thick shaft, running up and down a few times as if to show her he was harmless.

"It might not fit."

The words had simply tumbled out of her mouth but now that she'd said them she was kind of relieved. Spatial relationships weren't her strong suit, but he had to see that this simply might not be possible no matter how much she wanted it to.

Grinning, Travis rubbed his palms up and down her thighs in a comforting motion but all it did was send sparks straight to her sex. This man was turning her into a puddle of need.

"I'll fit just fine, baby. We'll take it nice and slow. There's no hurry. If anything hurts you stop me and we'll find another position that might work better. Are you ready for me?"

She'd been ready since practically the moment she'd met him but it didn't mean that she wasn't scared too. They were crossing a line in their relationship and there was no going back afterward. They could only move forward into the unknown.

And the unknown was terrifying as hell.

Aubrey felt him nudge her and instinct made her widen her thighs even as he pushed forward, gently but firmly, stretching her walls and drawing a gasp from her lips.

"Breathe, baby." Travis's hoarse words barely penetrated her befuddled mind, but she somehow managed a few ragged breaths as he continued to impale her until he was finally in to the hilt.

He didn't move a muscle, clearly waiting for her to give a signal that she was ready. His face a tight mask of control, his jaw rigid from the sheer will to hold back, he balanced above her on his palms watching her face for even the slightest whisper of discomfort.

But that wasn't what was happening. Heat was beginning to spread from her slit, through her abdomen, and down to her toes and fingertips. The strong urge to move couldn't be denied any longer and she experimentally swiveled her hips and a rush of pleasure suffused her entire body. Travis immediately picked up on the signal and slowly pulled almost all the way out before thrusting back in, his hips snapping against her own.

They set up a pace that was faster than slow but not frantic in its intensity. Her fingers gripped at his shoulders before sliding down his sweat-covered back to dig into his lean hips. Travis's head dipped down to capture a nipple with his lips and his thrusts took on a slightly different angle that had her seeing stars, moons, and asteroid showers.

"Like that, kitten?" he whispered into her ear, his voice a feral growl. "That's the spot, isn't it?"

It was indeed. A spot no one had ever found when inside of her before and she couldn't get enough of him stroking it, over and over until she was clinging to him, mindless with ecstasy and teetering on the brink of...something dangerous. Falling over the edge with him...letting herself go like that... Self-control at all times was what she'd depended on all these years, and if she wanted the glittery pleasure that was held just out of her reach she was going to have to let go and reach for it.

Travis didn't give her a choice this time any more than he had the first. He reached between their bodies to press his fingers against her swollen clit and her climax exploded, her entire body going taut and her toes curling. She heard herself call his name and then liquid heat ran through her veins until she was on fire from the inside out, barely cognizant of the world outside of the two of them.

She forced her lids open to watch as Travis reached his own peak, his head thrown back, his teeth snapped together. His incredible male beauty seemed more profound at an intimate moment such as this and she counted herself lucky to be able to see him – at the mercy of his pleasure.

He rolled off of her, taking her with him and tucking her into his side, one leg thrown over hers as they caught their breath. Aubrey's heart galloped in her chest as she came down from the most amazing high of her life. An addicting rush she already wanted to repeat again and again until she didn't know her own name.

"Are you okay? Did I hurt you?"

Travis's hands slid up and down her back and legs as if looking for some imaginary injury and she could only giggle in response. He worried way too much.

"I'm fine. In fact, I don't think I've ever been better in my life."

Where she'd found the courage – and the energy – to tease him she had no idea but he stayed still for a moment and then he pulled her more tightly to him, almost crushing the air from her lungs.

"Are you sure? You can't possibly have enjoyed that as much as I did. It was amazing. Stupendous. Life-altering."

"I'm sure, but I do have one little question."

Desire, arousal, and more than a little bit of mischief curled in her belly and she ran her fingers down his muscled arm, feeling every curve and dip.

"Ask away. You can have anything you want tonight."

That was good to know since she'd never felt more free in her life. Something had broken loose inside of her when they'd made love. She wasn't defective and this wasn't shameful or wrong. The way she felt for this man was beautiful and the things he made her feel couldn't be more right.

"So my question is this…when can we do that again?"

She heard him suck in a breath and then his chest shook with laughter. "I'm not as young as I used to be, so give me ten minutes. As much as I want you, maybe five. Damn, I'm not a teenager anymore but my body doesn't seem to know that."

The physical proof of that statement was currently stiffening against her thigh.

"If you need your rest–"

She didn't get to finish her sentence and instead found herself rolled onto her back, looking up at a very sexy and passionate man.

"Don't poke the bear, babe. There's a price to be paid for that."

His lips descended to press against hers and the last thought she had was that she'd gladly pay the price.

As often as possible.

Chapter Sixteen

TRAVIS SAT ON a barstool next to Tom Lovell drinking a Jameson on the rocks. He'd spent the better part of the day in bed upstairs with Aubrey, but they'd reluctantly stumbled out of bed in the afternoon when Shane came pounding on the door of the suite with more details about the land deal between Tom and Bruce. Not only had Bruce not paid a dime toward his debt, he had lured Tom into some high stakes poker games where the man had lost thousands. The fact that Tom had lost that money to someone Bruce also owed money to was an interesting coincidence.

Travis didn't believe in coincidences.

"Hell of a weekend. If I'd wanted this kind of hassle I wouldn't have bothered to leave Montana."

Tom snorted and tossed back his own drink, apparently tequila from the aroma and the limes and salt shaker sitting on the bar. "You're telling me. The cops wanted to talk to me again this morning. It's clear they don't know what the fuck they're doing. If everybody is a suspect then no one is."

"Did they say anything to you about who they really think did it?"

Travis had known Tom as an acquaintance for years, and although he wasn't a brilliant businessman he was intelligent. He'd graduated from Princeton with a degree in history and had knocked around his father's business for the last several years, but mostly lived off his trust fund. Now in his mid-thirties, he'd aged well and would be considered a handsome man by most women. He played up his natural good looks by dressing well and keeping in shape. His only bit of bad judgment seemed to be trusting Bruce in the first place.

"Didn't say anything to me." Tom tapped the bar and the bartender refilled the shot glass. "They asked me again where I was when Bruce was killed. If I liked or hated him."

From the slurring of Tom's words Travis could tell the man had been sitting at this bar for quite a while. Being inebriated would only help by lowering Tom's inhibitions and hopefully encourage him to tell more than he normally would.

"They asked me the same things too. What did you tell them?"

Tom grimaced and shrugged, knocking back another shot of tequila before answering. "I told them the truth. I was sitting with Alana. I was talking to her for quite a while actually."

"Was Martin there?"

Travis hadn't realized that Tom knew Alana well enough to sit and chat.

"No, he got a phone call and stepped out for a while. He asked me to keep Alana company while he was gone so she and I got some air outside for a few minutes."

That sounded like Martin, always the gentleman even when it was his birthday party.

"How long was he gone?"

Tom grabbed a handful of pretzels from the basket on the bar and shoved them in his mouth. "I dunno...a half hour maybe. Maybe more like an hour. Eventually Alana told me to ask her friend Tracy to dance. She was going to look for Martin."

If Martin had been on the phone all that time he had a good alibi as well, which made Travis happy. His friend had been through so much with Bruce he didn't need to be dragged through this murder investigation as well.

Sipping his own drink slowly, Travis was determined to stay as sober as possible. "It's good that you have a solid alibi. Did you see Bruce when he went out to the beach?"

Tom sucked on a lime after doing another shot. He was swaying now on his barstool and Travis had a feeling he was going to be helping the poor bastard back to his room in a short while.

"No. I saw him being a prick to some hot brunette. I could tell he was scaring her so I gave him some shit about it and told him to stay away from her. He just laughed and started dancing with Iris. That's the last I saw of him."

That hot brunette had to be Aubrey.

"He's lucky he had you to talk sense into him. He might have gotten in trouble with her husband or boyfriend. You and Bruce were good friends, right?"

"We've had our moments but for the most part we're friends. He owed me some money but he paid me back so that makes him a pretty damn good friend in my book. He also set me up with some business connections for my new cigar bar in Chelsea.

It wouldn't be happening if it weren't for him. He'll be missed. No one should go out that way, man."

Travis schooled his features so his reaction wouldn't show. According to Jason, Bruce hadn't paid Tom back. But who would know better than Tom himself? Would he lie? Certainly he might not want to be seen as having a motive, although it sounded like he lacked opportunity to begin with.

Shit.

"Let me know when it opens and I'll fly in to take a look."

Tom seemed to perk up at the subject. "It's going to be first class all the way, Travis. Mahogany bars. Top shelf booze. Hand rolled cigars. I have a connection in Ybor City over in Tampa for them. They'll be as close to Cuban as I can get without getting my ass in the slammer."

"It sounds like a winning idea. I'm sure you'll be very successful."

The conversation lagged as Tom did a few more shots and Travis nursed his whiskey. Finally Tom slapped the shot glass on the table.

"That cop can question us all he wants, but I know who killed Bruce. I know who did it."

It was stated with such certainty. Travis tensed as he waited for Tom to keep talking, not wanting to interrupt this spontaneous declaration. Tom leaned closer as if not wanting the bartender to overhear.

"Bruce was using information from the companies he researched to play the market. That's how he had the money to pay me back. Martin found out about it. I heard them arguing before the party. They both disappeared about the same time too."

How the fuck did Tom know about the insider trading?

"But you said Martin took a call," Travis reminded him. Just because Tom had suspicions didn't mean anything. The man was falling down drunk.

"That's what he said he was doing. But I never heard his phone go off and when he got up from the table he had it in his hand. I got a good look at it. His phone was off. Completely dark. No way did he get a call. I told that detective guy about it and the argument."

Son of a bitch.

Travis quickly finished his whiskey and threw down some cash on the bar. "I have to go, Tom. Do you need help getting back to your room?"

The man chuckled and raised his glass in a mock salute. "Naw, I'm going to stay here and keep drinking. Come back by later. I'll be here."

Exiting the bar area, Travis headed straight for the elevator.

It was time to have a private chat with Martin.

123

Chapter Seventeen

FEELING HAPPIER THAN she had in a long time – possibly her entire life – Aubrey quickly finished applying her makeup and packed it all away in her cosmetic bag. At home she would have left it all strewn across the vanity, but she was trying to keep her mess to a minimum since she and Travis were sharing a bathroom. All of his things were stowed in a small black case on the marble counter. Her toiletries, on the other hand, wouldn't even begin to fit there. She'd never thought of herself as all that high maintenance but compared to Travis she was traveling like a pack mule.

Surveying herself in the mirror, she noticed a sparkle in her eyes and a flush in her cheeks that hadn't been there before. They didn't owe their existence to any cosmetic company.

It was the face of a satisfied and happy woman.

Last night had been more amazing than she'd ever believed possible. Better than anything she'd read in a book, Travis had shown her the pleasure her body was capable of. She couldn't wait until tonight to do it all over again.

He was currently downstairs in the bar trying to get Tom Lovell to tell them anything that might help find out who had murdered Bruce. Honestly Aubrey was beginning to become discouraged about ever finding the real killer. It was beginning to look like she might be stuck here for weeks or even months while they investigated. She hadn't liked the way Prather had looked at her as if she ran around sticking knives in people she didn't like.

She heard the lock mechanism in the suite door and her heart clenched in her chest at the thought of seeing Travis again. It was silly and juvenile as he'd only been gone about an hour, but she couldn't contain her joy at being near him.

Her heart sank slightly when Shane walked through the door. "Did I scare you? Travis gave me a key since my room doesn't have much in the way of amenities. I had to take what they had left when I got here."

"You didn't scare me." She beckoned to him and he closed the door behind him before sliding behind the bar to fix himself a soda. "I just thought you were Travis. He must still be downstairs."

"Probably. Do you want one too?" Shane pointed to the can of soda on the bar and she nodded yes. "Actually I was here to talk to him about Iris Perry. I have a little more information about her."

Aubrey accepted an icy glass from Shane and then sat on the couch, her legs tucked underneath her. She'd chosen another simple sundress for today and the air conditioning was cool on her bare legs. "Anything interesting? Talking to her yesterday was strange. She seemed completely out of reality."

Shane settled himself on the adjacent sofa cushion. "I'm kind of surprised by that as well. Nothing in her personal history indicates that she has psychological issues. If anything it would be the opposite. She worked hard in school to get good grades, worked hard in her career and climbed the ladder until she became an assistant to a powerful businessman. That's how she met Bruce."

"He was doing business with her boss?"

"He was doing research on the firm for Martin. It looks like they hit it off right away and have been seeing each other on and off since then."

Aubrey shuddered, her lip curled in distaste. "Is it wrong of me to feel kind of sorry for her? Bruce was never known for being a very sensitive or even nice guy. It's hard to believe he was good to her."

Shane chuckled as he studied the contents of his glass. "It depends on what her goal was. If it was true love? I'm guessing it was a complete failure. If it was money? She hit the jackpot. Before she met Bruce she lived in a rat-infested four-story walk up apartment with three other women. Now she lives alone in a lovely two-bedroom on the West Side. Plus she owns a timeshare in St. Augustine, Florida. She definitely moved up in the world."

Whistling between her teeth, Aubrey moved restlessly on the couch. So many questions and hardly any answers. "Travis said that she was probably holding Bruce's money from the illegal trading. It sounds like she spent some on herself."

"Someone else was benefiting though. Every two weeks she made a wire transfer to a numbered bank account in the Cay-mans."

"Was Bruce planning on running away?" Aubrey set her half empty glass on the coffee table and stood, too keyed up to stay still. "Do you think he was going for some big score and then he and Iris would make a run for it?"

Rubbing his stubbly chin, Shane shook his head. "If I were to guess I would say that he was planning to make a run for it before the authorities figured out what he was doing. But I doubt he was planning to take Iris. I think she was meant to be left holding the bag, so to speak. There's no honor among thieves, my dear. None at all. They'd throw each other under the bus for a little financial gain."

The whole thing was sad. "Poor Iris. She sounded like she really loved him, although it's hard to believe. Still, there's someone for everyone I've heard."

"Honey, I'm not sure you need to feel sorry for someone that in all probability knowingly broke the law and profited from it. Not to mention she was sleeping with a married man. A married man with a very sweet wife. Bruce couldn't pull the 'my wife's a bitch' card with Iris. Caroline's one of the nicest people I know. She sure as hell didn't deserve to be treated this way."

"I didn't realize you knew her so well. Did you used to date her?"

Everyone in Tremont knew that Shane Anderson was an inveterate womanizer. An unapologetic one too. He made no secret of his admiration for the fairer sex, nor how much he enjoyed the pleasure of their company. His declarations of staying single and free sounded sincere and Aubrey had no doubt that he meant every word.

"Caroline?" Shane laughed, that Anderson dimple peeking out of his right cheek. "She's a friend but there's never been anything between us. We're like brother and sister. I feel the same about her as I do about you."

"She's going to have a tough time of it."

"Caroline will be okay. She's coming out to the ranch for a while. Travis's mom and dad and my parents will cluck over her like mother hens. They'll spoil her rotten like they never did their own kids. Hell, Dad would have us out chopping wood in the middle of January."

"I'm sure it built character," Aubrey teased with a smile. Travis had told her plenty of stories about the crazy adventures of the Anderson clan. "Did you walk five miles to school in the snow? Both ways?"

"With no shoes," Shane replied outrageously, his grin growing wider. "Seriously, Mom and Dad were tough on us. Travis had an especially hard time."

It made sense as Travis was the oldest of the four children and all the cousins. "He seems to have weathered it all right. Both of your parents are wonderful people."

"Hey, they didn't beat or starve us or anything." Shane drained his soda and hopped up to refill his glass at the bar. "They loved the hell out of us. But they expected us to work hard on the ranch and work hard at school too. Sports and clubs were encouraged and good grades were a must. You know the old saying about to whom much is given much is expected? Well, that was our childhood. They made sure we knew how damn lucky we were and didn't take it for granted. I know it couldn't have been easy to, either. I think they fought their natural inclination to make our lives easier than theirs had been, to give us all the things their newfound wealth could provide. I have to give them credit that they didn't turn us into entitled spoiled assholes. But it was Travis that really had all expectations of greatness on him. He knew from the day he was born he was meant to take over the family business."

"You all work in the business to some extent, even West and Jason in their way."

"Sure, but Travis is the lead. The brains. He's what makes Anderson move forward. Our dads are pretty much retired now and it all rests on Travis's shoulders. It's a big responsibility. He can't do the stupid shit that the rest of us do. He never could."

Shane held out a fresh drink to her and she took it, her mind still ruminating on his words. "What do you mean by stupid shit? Travis told me he's something of an adrenaline junkie and some of the things he's done are dangerous."

"The head is heavy that wears the crown," Shane quoted, leaning against the bar. "He's always known that he can only go so far. He can only get so crazy. He has to be the responsible one. The hardworking one. There was no year off after college and before graduate school so Travis could have one last hurrah or fucking find himself. Shit, by then he was working twelve to fifteen hour days between the office and classes. I have no idea how he found time to have a life, or even if he did, really. I was still in high school at the time."

Travis was a smart man who worked relentlessly for the family firm but Aubrey hadn't given much thought to what he'd had to give up to do that. "It sounds like he missed his childhood."

"In a way he did, but don't worry—we all had a great time when we were kids. His was just…a little different. There was no sitting around and fantasizing about being an astronaut or a rock star. His path was clearly written."

"That's too bad," Aubrey said softly, her heart aching for a little boy with a man-size future. "That couldn't have been easy for him."

"Don't feel sorry for my cousin, Bree. He has a great life and he'd tell you so himself if you asked him. Hell, until you came into the picture he had a different woman–"

Shane broke off and rolled his eyes, his cheeks turning red. "Shit. Fuck. I think I better shut up now."

She couldn't help but laugh at his shame-faced expression. "You don't have to tell me about the females in his life. I've been his assistant longer than his girlfriend. When I first started working for him the phone rang all day and it was a different woman every time trying to talk to him. Some even stopped by the office hoping to push their way in. Each and every one of them was completely gorgeous."

"And none of them meant a damn thing," Shane declared, his tone brooking no argument. "Travis was playing the field but those women never had a chance. But when he met you? He fell hard, honey. If you don't want him, please tell him now because he's fixing to start planning a future with you. What Travis wants he usually gets."

"I do want him. Very much." The conversation from the other night was running through her head. "He said something about how other women never saw the real him. That they didn't want to."

"We've all had our share of women who only have their eye on the Anderson money. Travis probably more than most. I have a feeling you don't care about all that."

She didn't and she hoped Travis would always believe in her. She cared about him, not the money or the power.

"Is that why you're not married? Have you had one too many gold diggers in your life?"

Something flickered across Shane's expression but it was gone so quickly she thought she might have imagined it. "I love women, and if you get married they frown on continuing to date and sleep with other females."

There had to be at least one woman out there that had tempted this handsome man to give up his bachelor card. "Then you've never been in love? That's kind of sad, Shane. Everyone should have love."

A muscle ticked in his jaw belying the carefree smile he wore on his face. "There are all different kinds of love, honey. Believe me, I don't spend too many nights alone in my king-sized bed."

He was obfuscating the subject to keep from telling the truth, and not doing all that good of a job of it. "That's not what I was talking about. Sex doesn't count. I mean, has there ever been a woman that made you want to be with just her?"

Shane was quiet, rubbing the back of his neck and looking off into the distance as if he was thinking about something or someone a long time ago, but then he shook his head. "No. There's no one. And the world should rejoice about that. I'd be a lousy husband." His phone chimed and he pulled it out of his pocket. "Travis. He's heading to talk to Martin and he wants me to take another run at Iris. He saw her in the resort gift shop on his way to the penthouse. He thinks she might respond to a charming male who compliments her and buys her drinks. That is my specialty. Will you be okay here while we're gone?"

Why wouldn't she? These Anderson boys worried way too much. She'd been taking care of herself for a long time.

"I'll be fine," she assured him. "Is there anything I can do to help?"

Shane shoved the phone back in his pocket. "Monitor Travis's emails for something from Jason. He and Jared are trying to track down who Iris is sending the money to every month."

Aubrey didn't even want to know how Jason and Jared were doing that, but their computer skills had come in handy when West was hunting down Alan Morton.

"Will do. I'll send you a text if I get something. And Shane?" He paused with a hand on the doorknob. "Be careful. There is still a killer out there and we don't know why he or she is doing this or who their next target is."

The usually smiling man's expression turned serious. "That's good advice, Bree. Deadbolt this door behind me and don't let anyone but me or Travis in. Not for any reason. Got it?"

She flipped the lock after he shut the door behind him and leaned back against it. Sighing loudly, she let her head fall back against the gleaming wood, her eyes closed as she replayed the events of the last few days. She didn't think she was in any danger but she would be careful. She didn't want to give Travis anything else to worry about. He already had the difficult job of clearing her name as a murder suspect.

He was one hell of a man to stick beside her through all of this and she vowed to make it up to him when this was all over.

Hopefully soon.

Chapter Eighteen

TRAVIS SETTLED INTO a chair opposite Martin and poured himself a cup of coffee from the carafe on the table. They were sitting outside on the patio again, the sky overcast with more menacing clouds rolling in for the afternoon. The humidity had risen to an uncomfortable level and not even the breeze coming off the Gulf could keep the sweat from gathering on Travis's back, the cotton fabric clinging to the damp skin.

"You're wearing a troubled expression, my friend." Martin pushed a tray of cookies toward Travis. From what Caroline had said when she let Travis into the suite, food was still being delivered all day long by the resort. "Do you want to tell me why?"

Not knowing how to bring up the topic delicately, Travis simply decided to lay it all out on the table. He and Martin had never pussy-footed around one another. They had enough respect to be honest and this time needed to be no different.

"I talked to Tom Lovell, Martin. He said he saw and heard you arguing with Bruce before the party."

Martin appraised him over the rim of his cup, his face devoid of any emotion. "That's absolutely true. But then you can't expect a conversation to be pleasant when you're accusing someone of breaking the law. Bruce was angry and defensive and I didn't hold onto my temper." The older man leaned forward. "Is there a reason you're bringing this up? If there is something you want to say, then say it."

"I can't fucking help you if you aren't truthful with me," Travis growled. "I want to find the real killer but you being vague isn't helping things."

"All you had to do was ask. Yes, Bruce and I argued. Of course we argued. We don't like each other and haven't since the first day I met him. You know as well as I do that I had motive for killing him. But I didn't do it."

Stirring his coffee, Travis didn't let up on the pressure. He needed to know it all. "Tom said you left the table to take a call but that your phone was dead or turned off. Where did you really go?"

The formally emotionless expression Martin wore turned embarrassed, his cheeks ruddy as he rubbed his right temple. "Shit. Okay, yes, I lied about there being a phone call. I was meeting Bruce out on the beach to continue our conversation. When I threatened him with exposure he said that he would name his accomplice which I assumed was Iris Perry. Then we were interrupted so we agreed to meet on the beach during the party around eleven."

This was bad. What else had Martin lied about? Obviously Prather knew nothing about this or he would have already arrested Travis's friend. "What did you talk about? Did you argue again? Was anyone else there?"

Martin shrugged, his lips pressed tightly together so they

were a thin line. "We didn't talk about anything because he wasn't there. I waited about ten minutes then went up to his room to find him. He wasn't there either so I came back to the party. I didn't see him again."

"Did you tell the police?"

"Are you kidding?" Martin scoffed, his movements agitated at the suggestion. "If I told them they would have slapped the cuffs on me and tossed me behind bars. No, it's better this way. Eventually they'll move on from me and find who really did it."

For a man as smart as he was, Martin was incredibly naive.

"I think you're being overly optimistic. I've seen people who live under a cloud of suspicion for years and it ruins their lives. That's why I won't wait around for the police. I'm going to work my own investigation." Travis clanged the spoon on the side of the cup. "Let's not even mention what will happen if the cops find out you're lying. They'll make your life a misery, ripping it apart and exposing it to the public. No one can stand that kind of scrutiny. They and the press will make a meal out of every little thing you've ever said or done."

Wringing his hands together, Martin nodded, hopefully understanding what Travis was trying to tell him. This could get serious very quickly.

"What can I do to help you?"

"You said Bruce had a bookie. I need his name. He had more motive than anyone to do this."

"I don't know but it's probably in the file the investigator gave me. It's in the bedroom."

Martin rose and entered the suite, leaving Travis out on the patio. The sky had turned almost black and the distinct smell of rain was in the air. He also stood and went back inside as Alana was coming through the door, shopping bags in hand.

"Travis! It's so lovely to see you." She dropped the bags on the couch and then reached up to kiss him on each cheek, European style. The aroma of expensive perfume assailed Travis's nostrils and he had to take a step back to keep from coughing. "Where's Martin?"

As if on cue Martin joined them in the living room, a manila file folder under his arm. Without making a big deal about it he slipped it into Travis's hand while greeting his wife with a kiss. "Looks like you've been busy, sweetheart. Did you have fun?"

Alana waved her hand in the air, the nails perfectly manicured. Travis didn't have a clue how she were able to do anything with long claws like that. Aubrey kept her nails fairly short with just a light pink polish that was barely noticeable. "It was fine. The stores here simply cannot compare to New York or Paris though. Tracy and I did have a nice lunch at a little bistro down the street. Are you big, handsome men talking business again?"

"You caught us," Travis smiled widely, glad she wasn't asking too many questions. "You know how we are. We just can't leave it at the office."

"I admire your dedication." Alana placed her hand on her husband's arm and gave him a big smile. "We should all have dinner together tonight. Caroline too if she's up for it. We've been stuck in this hotel room for the last few days and getting out would be a good thing."

"I'll have to talk to Aubrey and Shane. They may have already made plans."

Travis hoped they had. After the awkward discussion he'd had with Martin today they both needed some time away from each other.

A knock on the suite door had Martin scowling at the interruption. "It's like Grand Central in here. Whatever happened to calling first?"

Travis didn't bother to answer since he also hadn't called first before showing up. Alana opened the door and Prather stood there flanked on either side by uniformed police officers.

"Ma'am." The detective nodded to Alana. "We're here to see your granddaughter, Caroline Livingston, please."

Alana paused, swallowing hard before looking at Martin who waved the officers in the door. She stepped back and the three men strode into the room, Prather leading the way.

"Is she here?"

Martin shook his head, holding himself stiffly. "She's not. She went for a walk to clear her head. I don't know when she'll be back."

"Do you mind if we wait?"

Martin's jaw tightened. "I do, actually. She could be gone for hours."

A ghost of a smile passed over Prather's face. "Or five minutes. That's fine. I'll leave these two officers in the lobby. When she gets back to the hotel they can bring her down to the station. I thought she'd be more comfortable here…"

Martin grunted and pulled his phone from his pocket. "I'll try calling her."

"Thank you, Mr. Guinness. We do appreciate your cooperation. We have a few questions for you too, as a matter of fact.

5

Perhaps we can chat while we're waiting for your granddaughter to return."

Prather turned to Travis as Martin spoke softly in the phone. "I'm glad you're here, Mr. Anderson. I was going to call you. It seems that several eyewitnesses place Ms. Grayson in the ballroom at the time of death. Good news, your girl is off the hook."

Travis had wanted to clear Aubrey's name and it was a relief that her nightmare was over.

But he hadn't wanted suspicion to swing to anyone else he cared about.

This case wasn't over.

✦   ✦   ✦

SHANE STOOD IN front of a display of stuffed teddy bears with the resort logo emblazoned in the tummy, acting as if he was a legitimate shopper. The real reason he was standing there, however, was it was the perfect vantage point to spy on Iris Perry as she thumbed through a rack of tie-dyed dresses. Travis had wanted him to take a shot at befriending her and see if she would talk. Shane had no doubt he could charm her into a drink, but from what Aubrey had said the woman was in deep denial about her boyfriend's death. That didn't bode well for extracting any helpful information.

Shane was almost sure that she was eyeing him when he wasn't looking directly at her, and he was definitely sure when she worked her way through the shop until she was right beside him. With a hidden chuckle, he grabbed two bears off of the shelf and held them up.

"What do you think? The blue one or the brown one?" He

gave her a dazzling smile that had melted the panties off of more women than he could count. Iris's eyes widened in surprise, but then she smiled back and even fluttered her eyelashes. "It's for my niece and I'm hopeless at choosing gifts. I'd appreciate your opinion."

Her hand reached up to smooth her auburn hair before it came to rest on the brown bear, mere inches from his own.

"The brown definitely. So traditional but very adorable. How old is your niece, Mister…?"

"Just call me Shane." He leaned closer, invading her personal space slightly. When she didn't pull back he knew he had her interest. "Abigail is five and I always promise to get her something from all my business trips."

He placed the blue bear back on the shelf, letting Iris hold the brown one. "What business are you in, Shane?"

"Oil and mining," he replied, knowing exactly the reaction he was likely to get and he wasn't disappointed. Iris wet her lips, her hand dropping from the bear and landing on his arm.

"That sounds very important. You must be a busy man so it's sweet that you take time out to shop for your niece."

Shane shrugged and did his best imitation of an "aw shucks" grin. "I could have one of my assistants do it I guess, but it just wouldn't be the same." He nodded toward the bar across the lobby. "I do have a few minutes between meetings. I don't suppose I could buy you a drink? You know what they say about drinking alone."

"It would be impolite not to join you," she breathed, her voice husky. "Right now?"

Absolutely right now while you're entranced by my charm.

"Just let me pay for this." Shane pulled another brown bear from the shelf. "Let's get one for you too. I think every pretty girl should get a new…toy."

Her cheeks turned pink and she giggled as he led the way to the cashier. This was almost too easy and he felt a little dirty as he paid for the two stuffed animals. Charming women out of their clothes had been a hobby since he'd turned fifteen and had his growth spurt to over six feet tall. But all the women in the world couldn't fill the empty space inside of him.

Only one woman could do that.

The cashier bagged his purchase and he linked Iris's arm with his own.

"You're a pretty smooth operator, Shane."

Iris didn't look like she cared much if this wasn't a grand passion or true love.

"You're not so bad yourself. Now let's get that drink."

He led her through the lobby and straight to the bar. A few drinks and Iris Perry just might tell him something useful.

Chapter Nineteen

"I NEED YOU to go to New York City and talk to that bookie. I already called to have them ready the corporate jet."

Travis pulled Shane aside while Aubrey was chatting with her sister on the phone. She'd been elated at the news that she was no longer under suspicion but of course sad that Martin and Caroline weren't out of the woods yet. As far as Travis was concerned Detective Prather wasn't thinking globally enough. He was concentrating only on the guests at the party. Bruce had far more enemies than just those people.

"I can do that," Shane easily agreed. "I wouldn't mind trying to talk to a few of Bruce's business associates either. He had to have pissed off dozens over the years, what with his winning personality and caring attitude. I'll fly out tonight. Are you staying here in Florida or heading back to Tremont?"

"Staying here for the time being. I hate to leave a friend when the shit has really hit the fan, if you know what I mean. I don't know if I can help him but I want to try. Martin has done so many things for me all these years. I'd like to pay him back."

Even now Martin was demonstrating amazing grace under pressure. Travis was more impressed than ever with his mentor and friend. Martin could have pulled the billionaire card and brought in a phalanx of attorneys, but instead he'd stayed open and accessible. The man was a class act.

"There's only so much you can do, Trav. You can't do the police's job for them."

"I'm only trying to help. I'm aware that most police officers are underpaid and overworked. I don't doubt that Prather wants the real killer, but his limited resources don't allow him to look further than the small pool of suspects right here at the party. He doesn't have the manpower to look elsewhere."

Shane tapped a note into his phone before shoving it back into his pocket. "Do you honestly believe the killer isn't here this weekend? It's a long shot. I agree with Prather on this one. Someone here had the best opportunity. The murderer is someone you know, maybe even someone you care about."

Travis glanced sideways, ensuring that Aubrey was still deep in conversation with Gigi. "Is this your not so subtle way of saying you think it might be Martin? I've known the man for over fifteen years and he's no killer."

"All I'm saying is that it could be one of your friends here at the party. Someone you like and respect. You need to prepare yourself for that and not let your personal feelings blind you as we find out more information."

There needed to be a change in subject. Now.

"Tell me what Iris said. Did you find out anything at all?"

Shane's brows shot up and he grinned like the cat that ate the canary. "She has a boyfriend. Another one. But she never said his name. I think he was the one she was talking about to Aubrey because she mentioned he was really good looking. She didn't have a lot to say about Bruce."

Finally some information that might be useful.

"Two men and she had drinks with you. She's sociable, I'll give her that."

"She was rather offhand about Bruce, didn't seem all that broken up that he was gone. She spoke of her boyfriend in admiring terms so I think she's just an incurable flirt. I got the feeling she likes the attention so I made sure to give her plenty."

"Dating a man like Bruce I can't say I blame her. I doubt he gave her much attention." Travis stroked his chin in thought. "Did she tell you anything about the unknown boyfriend?"

"He's old money," Shane shrugged. "She mentioned his family had money but she was vague about what he did for living. But I got the feeling he was here this weekend. But that doesn't narrow things down much. Not in this crowd."

"Could her boyfriend have been jealous? That's a powerful motivator for murder. He was jealous of Bruce and he killed him. It's a viable theory. If the boyfriend is here this weekend someone must have seen them together. I'll do some asking around while you're in New York."

Shane nodded toward Aubrey who was wrapping up her call. "What you really need to do is take that pretty lady out on the town tonight and celebrate her being cleared. If that's not an excuse to romance a woman I don't know what is."

"Not that I need a reason but that's a brilliant idea. I have an idea too that I think she'll love. Text me when you get to the city. You can stay at my apartment. I'll call the doorman and tell him to let you in."

Aubrey deserved moonlight, roses, and champagne. She'd

been under terrible stress these last two days and Travis wanted to give her a chance to relax and feel normal again.

But not too normal.

He also hoped that she was falling more in love with him after their night together. He sure as hell would never be the same. She was everything he'd hoped to find in a woman and if she didn't want him it was going to break his heart.

Shane headed toward the door but stopped to drop a kiss on Aubrey's forehead. Brotherly, and in no way romantic. "Make my cousin take you somewhere and treat you like a princess. No hanging around the room and ordering room service."

Aubrey laughed, her face lit up and looking more beautiful than anyone had a right to. He felt that now familiar band tighten around his heart but he didn't fight it, instead welcoming the warm rush of emotion. This was what love felt like and he was damn lucky to be given a chance to experience it.

"I like room service and movies but maybe we will go out tonight. I take it you won't be joining us."

"I'm off to the Big Apple, Bree, but I'll be back before you know it. Try and stay out of trouble, you two. I won't be here to supervise your activities," Shane teased.

There was more than one kind of trouble and Travis couldn't wait to get elbow deep in romancing his woman.

Anderson-style.

Chapter Twenty

TRAVIS HAD RENTED out an entire mini-amusement park for their celebration date. Just the two of them and a few acres of fun.

There was miniature golf, go-karts, water bumper boats, a batting cage, and two floors of video games. She couldn't wait to go kill a few zombies after eating her weight in pizza, cake, and soda.

"I didn't expect this but I love it."

She hadn't known exactly what to expect when he'd told her to dress casually but this was beyond any of her expectations. It was crazy but it was exactly what she would have asked for if she'd even known this was an option.

"I was hoping you'd like this. At first I was going to take you to a fancy restaurant and then maybe some dancing or a moonlit stroll down the beach. But then I thought about you and me, and honestly we're not traditional romance people. I thought you might get a kick out of this. It is a celebration, after all."

"How did you make this happen on such short notice?"

She shouldn't have had to ask. She'd seen him in action too many times over the last several months and she knew how he'd done it. Money.

It made the world go round and it certainly opened doors. Or closed them to the public in this case.

"I know a few people, some friends. Do you want to eat first or play a little bit? We have the place until one in the morning."

Aubrey looked around, turning her entire body three-hundred-sixty degrees to take in all her options. He'd given her quintessential fun on a platter but she still had to choose.

"There." She pointed to the go-kart track. "I'm going to kick your ass."

A slow smile spread across Travis's handsome face.

"Care to make it interesting, kitten?"

Might as well make it fun whether she won or lost.

She took a deep breath and somehow managed to look him in the eye so he'd know she was damn serious about this. "Winner gets to be the boss when we get back to the hotel."

He leaned forward and brushed a kiss over her cheekbone. "Just to let you know…I like to be called 'Master' when playing this particular bedroom game. Let's do this."

He looked so fucking sexy and he smelled so tantalizing Aubrey had to gulp down the lump lodged somewhere near her vocal chords. With just a smoldering look he had her dampening her panties.

"Let's go," she croaked, not sounding as cocky as she had the previous moment. Luckily Travis was already striding toward the go-kart track, leaving her to trail behind him questioning her wisdom in bringing out his competitive side. The Anderson boys – especially Travis – didn't like to lose.

At all. In fact, they'd do just about anything to avoid it other than lie, cheat, or steal.

The game was on.

After buckling on helmets and climbing into the low-slung karts, they took a few practice laps before going at it seriously. Travis took the immediate lead but Aubrey stayed right on his tail, looking for an opportunity to pass. Blocking all attempts from her to make a move, he managed to stay in the lead for fourteen laps with only two to go. She'd have to do something bold or she was going to have to eat her trash talk.

And get on her knees and call him "Master".

It wasn't that she was morally against it. Any consensual game that two adults played was fine with her but she had to admit the thought of having him at her mercy was rather intoxicating. But she wasn't foolish enough to think it was more than a one-time thing. Travis Anderson was the alpha male personified. He might let her *play* the boss but he *was* the boss.

But she didn't like to lose either and a childhood of scrapping and fighting for every little thing had made her competitive as hell. With a surge of adrenaline, she slammed the gas pedal all the way to the floor just as she came out of the turn, going high and barely missing the wall by inches. Travis had taken the corner tight, leaving her a wide berth to go around him and she didn't hesitate for a moment. It was reckless as hell, but even as the next turn loomed she didn't let off the accelerator and her go-kart shot forward until she and Travis were side by side.

Her heart slamming against her ribs, she leaned into the next turn not willing to give a millimeter of the ground she'd gained. They stayed just like that, completely even, all through the lap and now the finish line was up ahead. Now or never. Victory or defeat.

Her foot was all the way to the floor and the kart was flat out going as fast as it possibly could. Sweat trickled down her back and forehead, and she held her breath as both cars flew past the finish line, her vision slightly blurred so it was hard to tell if one bumper was a little ahead of the other. It had been a photo finish and she couldn't help but feel a sense of satisfaction and elation. Even if she lost it wasn't by much. She hadn't embarrassed herself and she'd shown him she wasn't a pushover.

The karts slowed to a stop and Aubrey hopped out, stretching her cramped body. She was going to feel this tomorrow but not nearly as much as Travis would. He'd practically folded himself in half to climb into his kart.

Pulling off his helmet, he grabbed her around the waist, lifted her off the ground, and spun around several times in his arms until she was laughing and dizzy.

"Put me down. We're going to fall in a heap on the ground." She slapped ineffectually at his shoulders but he was still grinning down at her like a loon. He must have won the race.

The two employees who were running the place tonight ran over and picked up the discarded helmets before pushing the karts off to the side of the track but Travis's attention was solely directed at Aubrey.

"Girl, you drive like a professional. Where did you ever learn to do that?"

"I could ask you the same question. I was brought up in Chicago. We're fighters, Travis."

Once again she wondered about the women he'd dated in the past. If he'd been dating females too prissy to drive a go-kart what in the hell was he doing with her?

"You're one hell of a woman, Aubrey Grayson."

"You're one lucky man," she retorted, her cheeks turning a fiery red. She could feel the heat rising in her face all the way to her hairline. "Now I think you should feed me."

"As my lady wishes." Travis stepped back and bowed low with a flourish. He straightened and held out his arm so she could place her fingertips on the back of his hand as if they were lord and lady in some medieval play. "Let us retire to the dining room for a brief repast."

Giggling, she allowed him to lead her into the building where a very pretty young girl was behind the food counter obviously waiting just for them. There was a large, gooey cheese pizza, mozzarella sticks, wings, cheese fries, and cold soda to wash all the sugar and fat down.

"If we eat all this they'll have to roll us out of the doors and back to the resort," Aubrey said, sitting across from Travis in a corner booth. He'd asked the staff to put on some music – not too loud – and now Luke Bryan was singing softly in the background.

"I wasn't sure what we'd be in the mood to eat so I told them to fix us a little bit of everything."

"Looks like they fixed a lot of food. But I'm up for the challenge." She ripped a chunk of fries from the cast iron skillet, the cheese stretching into a long string that she had to wrap around her finger. "This is delicious, but then everything is better covered in melted cheese."

They ate quietly for a few minutes, their mouths full of the delicious food. She'd filled her plate with a sampling of each dish and when she made it around to the hot wings she was shocked by just how fiery they were. Her tongue burned, the heat growing hotter with every passing second, invading her sinus cavity and tightening her lungs. Fanning the imaginary flames coming out of her mouth, she grabbed her soda glass and chugged it down, groaning when it was empty.

"Holy fires of hell! Those are spicy." She dabbed at a few tears with a self-deprecating chuckle. "My nose is running and I'm crying. I'm not used to food that hot."

"Shit, baby. I'm sorry." Travis offered her his own soda. "I ordered them hot without thinking. They had a nuclear option. I'm just so used to ordering wings with Jason and West. Are you okay?"

She slugged back his soda as well but nodded in the affirmative. "I am. I just wasn't expecting it. This night is simply full of surprises, that's all. Don't worry, cowboy. I won't puke on your boots."

Travis quickly and efficiently refilled their sodas from the beverage station and she drank down half of that one as well. "Steady there. You might want to try a bite of cheese stick. Milk products dampen the fire of spicy foods."

Needing no second invitation, she chowed down on the deep fried mozzarella and the burning sensation began to blessedly recede. "No more wings for me. I'll stick to these yummy cheese fries. I could eat these all day long and never get tired of them."

"I love watching you eat. You enjoy every bite. None of this only eating lettuce stuff or bitching about your diet. If you like it, you eat it. Full stop."

She didn't mention the time in the gym she was going to

have to put in burning this meal off. It would still be totally worth it.

"Can I ask you a question?" She couldn't help herself. "Why are you dating me? I know you said that you like the fact that I don't care about your money but surely you've dated women who eat. I mean everybody eats, Travis."

Travis chuckled and scooped up another slice of pizza. "You'd be surprised. I guess I've chosen the wrong women through the years." He gave her a flirtatious wink. "But I've fixed that problem. Now I only date gorgeous brunettes who eat cheese fries and drive like Mario Andretti."

When he made such a persuasive case who was she to argue? She finally pushed her plate away, her stomach pleasantly full. "So are you going to give me another chance to beat you? How about we go head to head playing a video game?"

"What do you mean another chance?" Travis's brows pulled together. "You won the race, fair and square."

This was news. "I did? I thought at best we tied and that you probably won. It was really close either way."

"I think *you* won. You're right—it was neck and neck. How about we call that a tie and we play some more to break it? Best two out of three."

"Fine, but I warn you that I grew up playing video games. My adoptive family had three sons who were addicted to killing zombies."

Travis flashed that grin again. "I grew up actually shooting things for food. I think I'll be okay but thanks for the warning. I'll even let you pick the game."

It only took a few minutes of surveying her choices before

she selected a post-apocalyptic quasi-military game that featured the undead in graphic detail. She was in video game heaven but Travis was as well. They were evenly matched and it was looking like another tie was in the offing. They finally called it and roamed the empty floor looking for their next challenge.

They found it in an air hockey table.

"Man, we had one of these when I was growing up." Travis's face was alight with a boyish grin. "I don't know whatever happened to it. I need to get one of these for the house. What do you say we give this a try?"

"I'll have you know that I grew up playing air hockey and pool, so don't think you have the advantage here," Aubrey warned with a giggle. "I won't take mercy on you."

"That makes two of us, kitten. Ladies first."

She worked up another sweat and the lead kept swinging back and forth until she finally scooped the puck from the table and held it up. "Can we just call it even? I think I've had all the fun I can take tonight."

Travis laughed and came around the table to take the puck from her fingers and toss it back on the table without another look. "I think that's a good call. When the games are this close it might not be a good idea for either one of us to win. There's one more thing we need to do tonight but don't worry—there's no competition, baby."

She watched as he stuck his head in the kitchen where the lone female worker had been napping while they played. He strode back to Aubrey with a cocky grin and his arms wide open.

"May I have this dance? We are celebrating, after all."

The background music was louder and the song playing was

a slow ballad by Carrie Underwood. Aubrey slid into Travis's arms as if she was coming home. Her cheek was pillowed on his chest so she could hear the steady thud of his heart under her ear. His warm and citrusy scent wrapped around her like a downy comforter and she exhaled slowly, letting every muscle in her body relax against his hard frame.

He hummed in response and pulled her closer if that was possible, their feet moving to the slow tempo. Her hands fanned out on the broad muscles of his back as if trying to caress as much of it as she possibly could at one time before sliding to the waistband of his jeans, her fingers hooked into a belt loop.

"Are you disappointed, baby?"

The deep gravel of his voice vibrated against her skin and she looked up to see him regarding her with a tender loving expression that made her heart race and her palms sweat.

"With what? Everything is great, Travis."

His lips twisted and red streaked his high cheekbones. "Maybe you would have preferred to get dressed up and go somewhere fancy. I was just hoping that this was something different and fun. Something I bet you've never done with any other guy. But now I'm thinking that I didn't really consult you and that you might have wanted to do something very different. Did I blow it tonight? You can tell me the truth. If I did, I promise to make it up to you. Tomorrow night I'll take you anywhere you want to go."

She braced her hands on his biceps and leaned back so she could gaze into his moss green eyes. "This was perfect. I didn't have to dress up and mind my manners. I got to play games and kick your butt, eat junk food, and now I'm in your arms and dancing with you. I can't imagine anything better."

That eyebrow quirked up and he looked relieved. "Are you sure you can't imagine anything else? Because I have a few ideas."

Aubrey glanced over to the girl behind the food counter who was resting her chin in her hands, trying not to fall asleep. If Travis was thinking what Aubrey hoped he was thinking they didn't need an audience, even if the audience was snoozing most of the time.

"Can we go back to the hotel?" she asked boldly, her stomach already fluttering at the thought of being with him again. The passion and pleasure he'd shown her was an addictive drug. "I want to be alone with you."

His lips came down on hers, hot and hard, leaving her trembling in its wake. "Baby, let's get out of here. I have plans for your delectable body."

Aubrey had a few plans of her own. Last night had given her the confidence to know she could please him in bed. Now she wanted to do it – and a few other things she'd been fantasizing about – again.

They had on way too many clothes.

Chapter Twenty-One

AUBREY COULD BARELY contain her excitement as they sat side by side in the limousine heading back to the resort. Travis's warm body was pressed against her side, sending tingles to her private parts and making it hard to take a deep breath. Images from the night before crowded out any rational thought, leaving only raw emotion behind.

Of their own volition her fingers stroked his denim clad thigh, feeling the muscles jump and shift just from her touch. A growl was torn from his lips and his own hand clasped hers, holding it still.

"Do you know what you're doing, little girl? I'm on the edge here so you might not want to poke the bear."

There was clear warning in his tone but tonight she felt recklessly free and uninhibited. She'd never taken joy in her own sexuality before and it was far past time to do so. She wanted to celebrate the gift that only this one man had given her. Others could have done it in the past, but for whatever reason they didn't. Only Travis had the patience and care.

With her free hand she reached across her body and poked him playfully in the ribs, not trying to hide her glee. "Did you see what I did there? I poked the bear. What are you going to do about it?"

Travis actually looked shocked. As if no one had ever made fun of him while he was in this mood.

This was going to be more fun than she thought. This wealthy playboy businessman needed to take himself much less seriously and she was here to help him with that. She'd enjoy it too.

"You have no idea what you're doing." Travis leaned forward and hit a button. The dark divider between driver and passengers slid into place, providing the two of them privacy from any prying eyes. "You're treading on dangerous ground."

She certainly hoped so. Never in her life had she initiated lovemaking but she wasn't going to let her fear get in the way. "I've never done that before so I'm kind of looking forward to it."

His hand insinuated itself between her back and the seat until he was tugging on her hair, tilting her face so she had to look up at him. He didn't look angry but he wasn't smiling either. "Actions have consequences. Are you sure you want to go there?"

Their lips were a mere breath apart and she purposely pushed away that annoying little warning voice in her head that said to be a good girl.

Been there, done that.

"I think I want to push some boundaries. Cross some lines. How do you feel about that?"

Her fingers shifted until her hand sat directly on top of his hardening length. She heard his sharp indrawn breath but his hips lifted slightly as if to press himself more firmly into her palm. She immediately took the hint and caressed him through the denim of his pants before becoming frustrated, tugging at the buttons of his fly.

Hissing as her fingers found skin, he stretched out his long legs and positioned himself on the seat so that she could get a better grasp. He was hot, hard, and much more than a handful but she tightened her grip and ran it up and down the shaft until he groaned, his head falling back on the seat, his eyes closed with the onslaught of pleasure.

Checking once more to make sure the driver couldn't see them, she dropped to her knees in front of him and tugged his pants and boxers down far enough that he sprung free. A glistening drop of pre-cum was already decorating the reddish-purple tip and she swiped at it with her tongue, drawing a tortured moan from Travis and giving her confidence a much-needed boost.

His hands reached for her but she captured his wrists and shook her head. "No, I want to do this. Will you let me?"

Travis regarded her steadily, his gaze taking in every detail of the scene before him. She could only imagine what she looked like on her knees, her hair disheveled and her skin flushed with desire. "You don't have to do anything you don't want to."

"I know that but this is something I want to do. Not because I think you expect it and not because you want it. I'm doing it because the thought of it turns me on."

Apparently she'd spoken the magic words. He relaxed back in the seat and let her take control. He wouldn't allow it for long but he seemed content for now.

Aubrey ran her hands up and down his thighs, pushing them

apart as far as his jeans would allow. She gripped his shaft, caressing it from root to tip as he hissed and groaned. She rolled his sac between her fingers as she eased her mouth around the mushroom head, her tongue stimulating the sensitive spot just underneath. His hips jerked and he pressed farther into her mouth, bumping the back of her throat. Her eyes watered at the intimate invasion but she consciously relaxed her throat and jaw to take him as deeply as she possibly could.

Her panties were soaked and she had to brace herself on her knees well apart to keep from toppling over, she was shaking that hard. She'd set up a slow rhythm, keeping her mouth tight, moving her head up and down so as to simulate a good hard fucking as closely as possible.

His fingers tangled in her hair, his hands guiding her motions but she didn't take the time to chide him for trying to take control. She'd known it would be only a matter of time. With his urging she sped up, concentrating on the tip and using her hands on the lower half, her fingertips tracing the blue and red veins that stood out in stark relief to the velvet covered length. He was a beautiful man and this part of him was no exception.

His balls had tightened against his body and his breathing had become more ragged. She knew he was close so she wasn't prepared for his strong hands to lift her up and off until she was deposited on the seat next to him, his arms wrapped tightly around her body and his chest heaving with the effort to take a single breath.

"Why did you stop me?"

"Because I want to be inside of you," he whispered into her ear, his warm breath caressing the sensitive flesh there. "Because I want to look into your eyes when you come apart. You're so damn beautiful, baby."

If she hadn't been wet before his hoarse confession she'd be drenched now. Reaching under her short cotton sundress she tugged her panties down, one of the leg openings getting stuck on her sandals, but she managed to kick them off and let them drift to the floor of the limousine. His own hands were caressing her breasts through the thin material of the bodice and his trembling fingers went to the hidden zipper under her arm. He groaned as the dress parted, revealing her bare breasts to his hungry gaze.

His shaft pressed into her damp slit and she could feel it pulse in time with his heartbeat, sending frissons of pleasure straight to her clit. Bending his head, he captured an already erect nipple in his mouth. He nipped and tugged at the engorged flesh until she was writhing on top of him, white hot heat sweeping through her veins.

"Now," she breathed, her nails digging into his thighs. "Please, now."

"Are you ready for me?"

His voice, dark as a midnight sky, sent a shiver down her spine. Someday she might be able to come just from him speaking in her ear, making filthy, dirty, toe-curling suggestions. A thick finger slid deep inside of her and she threw back her head and moaned at the delicious invasion. She was so wet there had been no hesitation or discomfort and he easily added a second, moving them in and out and rubbing a sweet spot that had her quivering in his arms.

His hands gripped her hips and his thighs spread farther

apart, pushing her own even wider so she was at his mercy. She braced her hands on his shoulders as his steely length nudged at her entrance. Pushing into her slowly, his fingers tightened and the slight pain mixed with pleasure of being fully impaled by him made her head swim and her arousal build. By the time he was seated deep inside the walls of her channel were fluttering and gripping him tightly. She felt another rush of honey as he pulled almost all the way out, and then his hips snapped upward and she filled completely once again.

"Oh God," she whispered, leaning down to brace her forehead against his broad shoulder. "So good."

She didn't realize he'd even heard her but he snapped his teeth together, his jaw tight as he ground out, "It's never been better, baby. I want this to fuck you hard and fast so I can start all over and do it again and again."

That sounded good. Very good. Aubrey was on board for that plan. Now he just needed to get on with it.

"Yes, do it." Her fingers flexed impatiently on his biceps, needing Travis to do something…anything…dammit, he needed to move. "Don't make me beg."

He chuckled and began thrusting hard and deep but deliberate and slow. "You never have to beg, my sweet. I'm yours for the taking whenever you want me."

"Then fuck me now, cowboy."

Aubrey had never been so brazen, but then she'd never seduced a man in the back of a limousine before with a driver not four feet from where she was currently riding her sexy as hell boyfriend. She bit her lip to keep in her moans as Travis settled into a fast rhythm, his hips bucking underneath her like the broncos she'd seen him ride at the ranch.

Only he could last much longer than eight seconds.

Holding on for dear life, she arched her back and let her lids flutter closed as he thrust into her deeper and faster, finding the angle that made her crazy and stroking it again and again until she was teetering on the precipice, her orgasm shimmering just out of reach.

Travis reached down and pressed a thumb to her clit and her body's response was instantaneous. Like a bolt of electricity running from head to toe, her walls clenched around him as her orgasm took control. She bit into his shoulder to muffle her scream as her body trembled with the force of her climax. He found his own completion moments later, thrusting into her one last time, every muscle tense and rigid as he whispered her name as reverently as a prayer.

She collapsed on his chest with his arms around her like steel bands. The heavy aroma of sweat, leather, and sex hung in the air and she pressed kisses to the love bites she'd left on his otherwise smooth skin. If anyone saw them they'd know exactly what she and Travis had been up to.

His large hands cradled her head and he lifted her face so he could steal a long, slow kiss from her lips, their tongues dancing and rubbing until he groaned again, a laugh escaping from his firm, masculine lips.

"We better clean up and zip up, baby. We're almost to the resort. I'm sure our driver would love to get an eyeful of you but he might not be as thrilled to see all of me." He kissed her again, hard but brief. "I can't wait to get you back to our suite. I hope I haven't worn you out."

Giggling, she let her fingers run through his thick, springy hair. "Not in the least. There are several more things I want to do to you tonight. We are celebrating, after all."

"That's what I love about you, kitten. Your enthusiasm."

Aubrey didn't know if it was truly love yet, but if there was any man on this earth she could love it was this one. He was everything she'd hoped for and much more.

He was real, and solid and respectful.

And sexy.

She just might let herself fall in love with him.

It would be the most dangerous thing she'd ever done.

Chapter Twenty-Two

TRAVIS AND AUBREY paused outside of Martin and Alana's suite door. He gently squeezed her hand to remind her that it was simply breakfast. Martin might know that Aubrey had been a suspect but he also knew that she was in the clear. He certainly didn't know about the specifics of what Bruce had threatened and he need never know. Travis would take Aubrey's secret to the grave. Honestly it wasn't anything she should feel embarrassed about but it would take more than a weekend in Florida to convince her of that.

Hopefully they had a lifetime.

"Ready?" Travis asked Aubrey. She took a deep breath but nodded, shifting on her feet. She was dressed in a pretty flowered dress today and gold flat sandals. She'd pulled her long thick hair back with a barrette and it showed off the graceful curve of her neck and shoulders. Even after a night filled with lovemaking his body hadn't had enough. Like a hormone filled teenager he wanted her again.

Rapping his knuckles on the door, he leaned over to give Aubrey a quick kiss on the forehead and barely made it before Alana was there ushering them in and back out to the patio where they'd visited previously.

"Thanks for the breakfast invite." Travis sat down with Aubrey on his right and Martin and Alana across from him. "Is Caroline joining us?"

A frown flitted across Martin's features only to be replaced with anger. "She's still asleep. That damn detective questioned her for over two hours yesterday. Finally our attorney called a halt to the whole thing but by then she was so upset she couldn't get to sleep for hours. Alana finally convinced Caroline to take one of her Ambien pills which luckily worked."

Shrugging, Alana poured them all coffee from the large carafe. "My insomnia finally paid off in some way. Within a half hour she was out like a light. With everything she's been through she deserves a good rest. There's the room service."

Alana bustled back into the suite to let in the food delivery and Travis took the opportunity to lean closer to Martin. "Listen, I want to apologize about the last time we talked. I didn't mean to come off–"

"Don't give it another thought." Martin chuckled at Travis's discomfiture. "You're like me, son. When you're determined you make things happen and that's exactly what someone needs to do. Have you found out anything?"

"Shane's due back later today. He's been running around New York City trying to talk to the bookie and also to a few other people, so he hasn't contacted me."

"Which frustrates the hell out of you." Aubrey patted him on the arm. "He said if he had anything significant he would call. I think this just means that he hasn't learned anything that earth shattering."

That's what Travis was afraid of but there wasn't a damn thing he could do about it. Neither he nor Shane could force anyone to talk to them. As it was, they'd used some rather underhanded techniques to speak to people. Not that he regretted it. He'd do anything to clear Aubrey or any of his friends and family, but he'd only wished he could do it a little more out in the open.

Martin smiled kindly at Aubrey. "I'm sorry that you got caught up in this. I hate to speak ill of the dead but Bruce caused a lot of trouble in his life. Hopefully he'll find some peace, as we all will too."

"Thank you," Aubrey replied softly. "I hope your granddaughter is going to be okay. Being married to Bruce couldn't have been easy."

"Being his widow hasn't turned out to be much better." Alana was back on the patio directing the staff as to where to place the trays of food. "She's going to go through more hell before this over. Even in death he can't leave her alone."

The resort staff filed out but before Alana could close the door Detective Prather entered the suite.

"Detective, what can we do for you today? Caroline is asleep so if you want to talk to her you'll have to wait." Alana pointed to the resort hallway. "Somewhere else preferably."

Martin stood to join Alana inside and Travis and Aubrey followed, wanting to show support for their friend. It was a cluster the way Prather was conducting this investigation as if everyone was guilty as hell and it was up to them to prove themselves innocent. It was Prather's fucking job to find the guilty party, but he seemed unable to look past the fact that all the suspects were rich as hell.

Prather's eyes narrowed as he took in all of them enjoying their breakfast on the patio. "Actually, Mrs. Guinness, I'm here to speak to your husband. Mr. Guinness, have you ever seen this before?"

The detective pulled a plastic bag from his pocket that contained a small cufflink, black onyx with a diamond solitaire. Travis's gut tightened. He'd seen that cufflink before.

"It's mine." Martin reached for the bag and Prather let him take it to examine the piece more closely. "How did you get this?"

The detective smiled but it didn't reach his eyes. "I'm glad you asked that question. This cufflink was found underneath Bruce Livingston's body. We didn't have any idea who it belonged to until we found a picture of you on the Internet wearing this same pair. Do you have any explanation for that?"

"This has to be a mistake," Alana stepped forward and protested. "I'm sure there are other people with the same set. It could be anyone."

"Except that you were at the party," Prather replied. "Did you bring this set of cufflinks with you, Mr. Guinness? If these don't belong to you, can I see yours?"

Martin had been still but he came out of his reverie, shaking his head and ducking into the bedroom, calling behind him. "I'll get my set and you'll see that those aren't mine."

Aubrey's fingers curled tensely around Travis's arm and he didn't blame her a bit. They could hear Martin fumbling through drawers and a curse word here or there. It was hard to stay optimistic at the moment.

Martin stepped back into the living room, his mouth a grim line. He held up a single cufflink. "I can only find the one. The mate seems to be missing. I'm sure I'll find it."

"I think we already have," Prather stated flatly.

"I didn't do this. I would never take the life of another human being," Martin protested but Travis could see it wasn't going to work. The detective had made up his mind. "I wasn't even wearing those cufflinks the night of the party. I was wearing a different pair."

"Martin Guinness, you are under arrest for the murder of Bruce Livingston." Prather's recitation of Maranda rights was drowned out by Alana's shrill scream and she slumped against Travis, her eyelids fluttering and her lips trembling with the shock. Aubrey immediately stepped forward to comfort the weeping woman, helping Alana over to the couch so she could sit down.

The detective managed to finish informing Martin of his right to remain silent which it appeared the billionaire was availing himself of, his own skin a pale ashy gray. "You may want to phone an attorney, Mrs. Guinness."

Alana didn't look capable of doing anything at the moment. Her hand was over her mouth as tears ran down her unlined cheeks, the mascara streaking her face. As Martin was cuffed he turned to Travis.

"Call Barry for me, will you? And get Caroline to sit with Alana. I'll be in there until they can set bail."

"Will do. Don't worry about us out here," Travis assured his friend and mentor. "We'll have you out in no time."

Travis hoped. It was a murder charge and bail might or

might not be an option. The best action would be to prove that Martin was completely innocent.

This case wasn't over.

✦   ✦   ✦

AUBREY SIGHED AS she clicked through photographs from the party on Travis's laptop. Somehow he had managed to charm the official photographer into giving him a thumb drive with all the pictures from the night Bruce Livingston was murdered. There were literally hundreds to go through and every one had to be checked. They were hoping to be able to prove that Martin had been wearing different cufflinks just as he said.

"None of these photos of Martin show his wrists. They're either from the shoulders up or he's turned in the wrong direction."

Travis was at the dining table looking through the file on Bruce one more time. Snapping it shut, he came to sit next to her, his arm across her shoulders. "If you're tired and need to give your eyes a break I can take over. You've gone above and beyond today. This is my fight, not yours, sweetheart."

He truly believed that and she needed to disabuse him of that notion as quickly as possible.

She perched on her knees so she could cup his jaw in her hands and look directly into his eyes. He needed to see she was sincere about this. "If it's your fight then it's our fight. We're a team now—at least I thought we were. When you talk about your future am I just there for decoration? I want to be a real partner to you. I want to share everything and that means the work and the struggles, not just the fun and the wealth. If that's not what you have in mind then tell me, because when I picture us together it isn't me spending my days getting my nails done and shopping. It's loving you, being with you, helping you."

His hands caressed her spine and his expression softened, filling with a tenderness that took her breath away. "Sort of like for better or worse? Is that what you mean?"

Heat filled her cheeks at his intimation. She'd never presume to bring up a commitment like that this early in their relationship, but he just did and bravely too. She couldn't let him twist in the wind out there all by himself.

"Yes," she breathed softly, butterfly wings fluttering in her abdomen. "Kind of like that. But we're talking about the future, remember?"

His brow quirked and a smile spread across his handsome features. "So this is practice?"

"Repetition is the key to mastering a skill," she teased. "I think if we practice and get good at this for better or worse won't seem like much of a task at all. Can you share all of that with me, Travis? Can you open yourself up to showing me every part of your life?"

For a moment she saw indecision in his eyes and she actually felt a moment of relief. It meant he was taking this seriously and really thinking about what she'd asked him. It wasn't a trivial moment in their relationship and he realized it.

"I can do that." Travis nodded and pulled her closer. That one fleeting moment of insecurity was gone and all she could see in his face was happiness. "I want to do that."

"Good." She pressed a quick kiss on his lips. "Now let's get back to work. Notice I said you and me."

They were quiet as they paged through the photos, enlarging a few to see if they could get more detail. Somehow she had migrated to sitting between his legs, his back against the arm of the couch and the laptop propped on her knees. He nipped at her neck and earlobe, his arms tightening around her waist.

"Thank you."

"You're welcome, but I'm not sure what for."

There was a silence and then he whispered to her, his breath warm on her cheek. "I've never met anyone like you."

She smiled and giggled but didn't turn around, simply settling back against him more comfortably.

"I hope that's a good thing."

"It's a very good thing. The best thing that's ever happened to me."

Her heart skipped a few beats and she had to remind herself that this man wasn't like the others she'd known. He believed what he said. He wasn't saying it to get in her pants or because he thought it was expected. He said it because he felt it and that meant more than anything she could name.

"You too."

Her hands were on the laptop keyboard and he placed his much larger ones on top of hers before winding their fingers together. "I guess we need to stop making cow eyes at each other and get back to work. But how about we go see a movie tonight? There's a theatre not far from here. I think we could use the break to get our minds off everything."

Sitting next to Travis in the dark with popcorn? Yes, please.

"Do I get to pick the movie?"

Travis laughed and she could feel the rumble from his chest

against her back. "Yes, princess, you can select the movie. I suppose you're going to want junk food too?"

"You bet. Lots of it."

"Then we better get back to work. We have to find some evidence that exonerates Martin. I don't believe for a second that he did this. It just isn't in his nature."

Aubrey hoped Travis wasn't wrong.

Chapter Twenty-Three

TRAVIS AND AUBREY were returning to the resort about midnight after a late movie when he saw flashing lights just up ahead. By the time the taxi pulled under the canopied entrance Travis had counted at least three patrol cars and a fire and rescue unit.

"This can't be good."

Quickly paying the driver, Travis and Aubrey hopped out of the taxi and rushed into the lobby. There were a few clusters of people here and there but he clearly heard the words "pool" and "drowning."

"Let's go outside." Travis put his arm around Aubrey and led her out the back entrance and down the stone path to where a group of people had gathered around the edge of the large swimming pool. He was about to ask one of the gawkers what was going on when he saw Shane standing at the perimeter. Rounding the crowd, he nudged his cousin to get his attention.

Shane dragged his gaze back to Travis. "About time you got here. The shit has really hit the fan. Let's go up to the room."

Travis pointed towards the uniformed cops. "What's going–"

"Just trust me," Shane cut in. "I'll tell you what I know when we get upstairs."

Nodding, Travis placed his arm around Aubrey and they skirted around the edges of the crowd. When they reached the far side near the entrance the people parted for a moment and Travis could see a body on the ground covered with a blanket.

Shit, another body.

Remembering how upset Alana was earlier when Martin was arrested filled Travis with a sense of dread as they quietly slipped into the hotel and up the elevator. When they finally entered the suite Travis couldn't keep quiet any longer.

"Was it Alana? Goddamit, Shane. What the fuck happened? We were only gone for a little over three and a half hours."

Aubrey grabbed his hand and squeezed his fingers, giving him "the look". "Give Shane a chance to answer, babe."

Shane rubbed his chin and exhaled noisily as if not sure where to begin. Or maybe he was just trying to drive Travis fucking insane. Either one could be the case.

Shane walked over to the bar and retrieved a beer from the refrigerator. "I got back from NYC about an hour ago. Cab dropped me off and there was already a few people gathered at the back of the hotel. Not as many though so I had a good view of things. The body belongs to Iris Perry. It looks like she might have fallen into the pool and drowned. Maybe accidentally. Or maybe not. They'll know more after the autopsy."

Aubrey gasped and sat down on the couch, her eyes wide with shock. "Iris? Oh my God. She's dead?"

"Quite dead." Shane also sat down on the couch and stretched his long legs out to rest his feet on the coffee table. "The question is did she kill herself because her lover is dead?

Did she kill herself because she felt guilty about murdering that lover? Or…and this is the question I like…did someone help her drown? And did that person have something to do with Bruce's death?"

Travis raked his fingers through his hair and groaned. "Shit. What in the hell is going on here? Two murders in less than a week. That has to be a record for this establishment. Do Caroline and Alana know yet?"

"I don't know. I haven't seen them. I only took a few minutes to bring my bag upstairs and then I spent the rest of the time out back." Shane gulped down the last of his beer and slapped the bottle on the coffee table. "What are you thinking right now?"

Another good question.

"That I'm stunned by the turn of events and haven't quite wrapped my mind around what's happened. Iris's death brings up many more questions than it answers, I'm afraid."

"But it does clear up one thing," Aubrey offered as she kicked off her shoes and curled up on the sofa, her legs tucked underneath her. "Martin couldn't possibly have done this because he's in jail awaiting arraignment. Since the two deaths are probably linked I would say that's a compelling argument for releasing him."

Travis's chest puffed out with pride. "That's my girl. You're starting to think like a detective. You're absolutely right. If Iris died from foul play then Martin should be cleared from both deaths."

Her answering smile made his heart ache in his chest.

Shane groaned and rolled his eyes. "Can you two cool the

goo-goo eyes and kisses for just a few minutes? Should I leave you two alone?"

Aubrey grabbed one of the throw pillows from the couch and smacked Shane right in the face, much to his shock. "We were not kissing, although I'll admit to the goo-goo eyes. But you can't blame a girl. I was warned the Anderson men were lethal but I still couldn't resist."

She always knew what to say and this occasion was no different. Shane grinned and practically beamed with pride. He enjoyed his reputation as a ladies' man. Hell, he reveled in it.

"So back to the issue at hand." Travis steered the conversation to today's events. "It looks like we need to find out some details about Iris's death but I don't think Prather is going to be very forthcoming. He already has a shit attitude about pretty much everything."

Leaning forward, the throw pillow on his lap, Shane waggled his eyebrows as if he was the villain in a silent movie. "I'm already on that, cousin. There were reporters there and I talked to one of them who would be willing to give us some information as long as we promise to give him an exclusive regarding Anderson Industries. He says he has an in with the forensic team and the coroner. I think he's probably the best shot we have to learn anything."

"Not one lead has panned out," Travis groused, getting two more beers from the refrigerator and a soda for Aubrey. He handed the longneck bottle to Shane before opening his own. "You didn't learn shit in New York. The bookie wanted Bruce alive so he'd get paid. We can't find a photo of Martin's cufflinks the night of the party and no one we talk to seems to know a damn thing and yet everyone has a motive."

"Call Jason and West."

Aubrey's soft voice pulled Travis out of his frustrated misery. "What? Why?"

She looked almost afraid to answer as if he would be offended. "Because they're cops and they'll know what to do when we hit a dead end like this."

Shane grinned and slapped his thigh with glee. "Damn, woman, you're right. We're so entrenched in this mess we can't see what the hell we're doing. I'll get one of them on the phone right now."

"At least one of us is thinking straight."

Aubrey scooted onto Travis's lap and laid her head on his shoulder. His pulse sped up at the delightful female that was currently nestled against him. "You need to give yourself a break. First you were trying to clear me and now Martin. You're emotionally invested in this case and that doesn't make thinking clearly easy."

She'd brought up a salient point. Was he blinded by his respect and admiration for his friend? Martin had plenty of motive to kill Bruce but Travis honestly couldn't imagine the man doing it. If he couldn't keep an open mind and make logical decisions he wasn't going to do any better than Detective Prather.

Shane fished his phone from his pocket. "I'll call Jason. Or West. Wait, which one do you think will answer their phone?"

Travis had no doubt at all. "West. He told me that he keeps it on twenty-four-seven. It's a cop thing."

"But he's the mayor now." Shane was pressing buttons on his phone.

"I'm guessing the habit hasn't died."

It hadn't. West picked up on the second ring and Shane put the phone on speaker.

"Brother, we need your advice. We're at a dead end here and I don't know our next move."

"I've been there more than a few times," West laughed on the other end of the line. "When you don't know what to do next the best thing to do is go back to the beginning. Look at all your suspects again even if you think you've eliminated them already. Look at who had motive and opportunity, but especially opportunity. Just because you think someone doesn't have a motive doesn't mean they don't. It could be hidden, so don't think a person is innocent just because you can't see a motive. You need to make a chart of where everyone was at the time of the murder. Then take a closer look at anyone you can't account for. But basically it's all about going back to the basics. Don't overthink this, Trav. In most cases criminals aren't that bright."

Travis hoped that were indeed true.

Chapter Twenty-Four

T WO LARGE PIZZAS later Aubrey, Shane, and Travis were sitting around the dining room table. They'd cleared it completely and were ready to start at the beginning.

"So what do we know for sure?" Aubrey asked, placing a notebook and pen in front of her. "Let's make a list."

She tore out two pieces of paper. One she titled *Things We Know* and the other she titled *Open Questions.*

"We know that Bruce owed money to a lot of people," Shane offered. "We don't know if he paid Tom back or not."

"That's a good start." She scribbled details on her lists. "What else?"

Travis stood and looked out of the windows but the moon was hidden behind clouds tonight. "We know Bruce was stabbed in the heart. It suggests that the killer had to be able to get close. I doubt a stranger could get near enough to make the first strike deadly."

"He could have been surprised from behind and turned around," Aubrey pointed out, chewing on the end of the pen. "Maybe the killer never gave him a chance."

Shane shook his head. "I'm not buying that. Let me show

you." He tossed an extra pencil at Travis who caught it easily in his right hand. "I'll stand here and you come up behind me."

Shane stood with his back turned about five feet from Travis who stealthily snuck up behind Shane. Travis raised the pencil like a knife but at the last minute Shane spun around and grabbed Travis's wrist, and a mock struggle ensued with Travis finally dropping the pencil on the floor.

"According to our sources, there were no defensive wounds on Bruce's person which tells me he didn't see it coming. Unless he was deaf and blind I don't think he would have let a stranger sneak up behind him and shove a knife directly into his heart. But that's just me."

Aubrey sighed and held up her hands in surrender. "Mea culpa. I'm convinced. I see what you're saying and it makes sense. Only someone he wasn't afraid of would have been allowed to get that close without him fighting back."

"But is that something we actually know or just suspect?" Shane popped open another soda. "I don't think we can know it for sure at this point. We don't have any of the forensic reports to help us either which really ties our hands."

"We can't know it but I think we can call it an assumption. I don't think this was a stranger killing." Travis braced his hands on the back of a parson's chair. "Bruce was killed for a reason. This wasn't some random act of violence."

Aubrey scribbled more on her list. "I'll put an asterisk next to it to mark our assumption. What else do we know?"

All three were silent until Shane rolled his eyes and groaned loudly. "Shit, we really don't know anything, do we?"

"We know that my whereabouts were confirmed by other

people at the party, so that means we have a time of death or at least an idea. They think he was killed around eleven-thirty."

Aubrey tapped her chin with the pen. She'd always had a respect for law enforcement, but now they'd soared in her estimation if this was what they dealt with every day.

"Good." Travis rubbed the back of his neck as he paced back and forth. "Who else do we remember at the party during that time? We can take them off the suspect list."

An hour later they had a list of party guests they couldn't account for and possible motives they might have. Aubrey rubbed her temples and yawned, a headache pounding behind her eyes. It was clear she wasn't cut out for this detective stuff.

Travis sat down and leaned his elbows on his knees, his chin cupped in his hands. "But this doesn't even scratch the surface as to who would want both Bruce and Iris dead. That's the real mystery."

The faces of party guests drifted through Aubrey's mind but one kept crowding out the others.

"Caroline," she said softly. "She had motive to kill both of them."

Travis was already shaking his head. "I don't want to believe that. She's been through the wringer with Bruce."

"All the more reason for her to kill him," Shane retorted. "She's a sweet girl as far as we know, but hell, we don't spend that much time with her. Not really. She could have done it and she's on our list of people not accounted for during the time of death. We have to consider her."

Travis fell back into one of the chairs and dragged a hand down his face, stubble darkening his jawline. "Dammit. I know we have to. I just hate the thought of it. We also have to include Martin as well. He'd do anything to protect his granddaughter."

"Add Alana to that list," Shane offered with a grimace. "I personally don't know what Martin sees in her but she does appear to be in love with him. If she thought he was being hurt by Bruce with the insider trading thing, and by extension Iris as his accomplice, she might have killed them to help her husband."

Travis picked up two soda cans from the table and offered one to Aubrey. "At least you're off the list. You might have had a motive for Bruce but you didn't know Iris and had no reason to kill her."

That was true, but it felt strange to have had a conversation with a woman a short time before she died. Had it been only been two days ago? It felt like a lifetime had happened since then.

"West said you shouldn't worry about motive," she reminded him, accepting the soda and popping it open. She needed the caffeine desperately as it had been a long night.

Travis grinned and nudged her foot with his own under the table. "I'm pretty sure you don't have any hidden vendettas against Iris Perry, nor are you big enough to wrestle her into a pool and hold her down until she drowns."

Aubrey tapped her pen on the table as she pictured different scenarios. "What if she was drunk or drugged?"

"That might make it easier or harder." Travis raked his fingers through his hair for the dozenth time that evening. "She'd be dead weight if she was unconscious. No, I think it would take a man."

Shane stretched his arms over his head and twisted his head side to side in an attempt to shake off several hours of sitting. "Of course we're assuming that she didn't drown herself or that it wasn't an accident. I don't see the latter happening but possibly the former."

"She didn't seem very suicidal when I talked to her at the spa," replied Aubrey. "She wasn't even mourning really. That could be part of the denial maybe. It's all so confusing. Where do we go from here?"

Travis drank down the last of the soda and slid the can to the center of the table with the discarded pizza boxes. "Martin, Alana, and Caroline are our best bets as much as I hate to say it. Hopefully we'll hear from that reporter Shane befriended and find out what the forensic team and coroner have to say. Without that information we're flying blind."

Aubrey stood from the table and tucked the laptop under her arm. "I'll get back to work looking at those pictures from the party. Maybe we'll see something in them that will help besides just looking for a picture of Martin's cufflinks."

"It's late," Travis objected. "You should get some sleep."

"Are you going to bed?"

She knew he wasn't. He had that look on his face she'd seen so many times before.

"Shane and I are going to go through the file that Jason sent us regarding Bruce one more time. See if we missed anything."

No surprise there.

"Then I'm working too. Should I put a pot of coffee on?"

Travis opened his mouth to argue and then simply smiled. "I almost forgot about that team thing we talked about. Make it a strong pot, babe. I have a feeling we're going to be up all night. Or what's left of it."

Aubrey hummed as she measured out the coffee, her gaze straying to the man in her life every so often. She admired his dedication in trying to help her and now he was helping his friend as well. He could go back to the office and mind his own business, letting Martin rot in jail, but he wasn't the kind of man to do that.

He wasn't perfect but he was good. And kind.

She waited for the fear and trepidation to seep into her bones but it didn't come. It felt just fine and not scary at all. In six short months he'd managed to knock down years of defenses. He'd never given up no matter how many times she'd pushed him away.

She was ready to embrace being happy.

Now the only issue was making sure he felt the same.

He'd talked of the future. He'd even mentioned marriage.

Somehow she needed to find a way to tell him she was all in. Ready to take the next steps.

She was in love.

Chapter Twenty-Five

B LEARY-EYED AND LOUNGING on the sofa, Aubrey clicked through the remaining party photos one by one. In the past four hours she'd ingested three sodas, cold pizza, and a Snickers bar from the vending machine down the hall all in the hope of staying awake. So far it had worked but she wasn't sure how much longer it would. She was fading fast.

Shane was snoring softly on the other end of the couch and Travis was in the bedroom talking to Jason on the phone. The younger brother might know someone who could comment anonymously on the insider trading investigation.

Clicking on a photo of Martin and Alana's table, Aubrey sat up quickly and enlarged the picture so she could see more detail. She sucked in a breath and let it out in a rush when the cuffs of Martin's white shirt were revealed.

He wasn't wearing the onyx and diamond set either. Instead he was clearly wearing a plain gold pair that bore his initials.

Score.

Hopping up from the couch with a cry of delight, she ran into the bedroom still carrying the laptop, her fatigue a distant memory. It finally felt like something – anything – was happening with this case.

"I found it." She was practically bouncing up and down with excitement and Travis must have been exhausted as well, because instead of being happy he frowned and held up a hand, pointing to his phone.

"I'm talking to Jason. Can this wait, babe?"

Aubrey rolled her eyes and lifted the laptop so the screen was facing him. "No, it can't wait. I found it. I found a photo of Martin wearing another pair of cufflinks."

Travis's eyes widened and a smile spread across his face. "Uh Jason, can I call you back? My clever girlfriend looks like she's found something. Yes, I'll call you and tell you about it."

Tossing his phone on the side table, he took the laptop in his hands and sat down on the bed, patting the mattress next to him, and Aubrey joined him. She pointed to the photo on the screen, excitement in her voice.

"There it is. Proof positive that he didn't wear the onyx cufflinks to the party."

Travis's fingers glided over the keys. "Not exactly. If this photo was taken late into the evening he might have changed his cufflinks by then after realizing he lost one. If the picture is early in the evening it gives it more credibility."

"The mushroom appetizer is sitting on the table." Aubrey pointed to the screen and grinned. "That was very early in the evening. See? It does prove it."

"It helps prove it," Travis corrected gently. "I don't know if Prather is going to be swayed by this but it should at least help Martin's case, especially now that Iris is dead. He was already in jail when that happened."

"I'm still happy that I found it. It's a clue that exactly might mean something among all the things we don't know."

Travis placed the laptop on the bed and wrapped his arms around Aubrey. She settled against him, his warm scent enveloping her senses while the heat from his body penetrated the thin cotton of her pajamas. Her heart kicked into high gear at his nearness and she could feel his own thudding against her cheek. Her fingers curled around his biceps, the muscles firm under her palms. She'd been up all night but suddenly sliding in between the sheets just to sleep didn't seem all that inviting.

"You did a great job." Travis's praise warmed her inside and out. When they were working together he didn't go overboard with compliments but when he gave one it was truly sincere. As a child she hadn't received much praise and it was kind of pathetic that it meant this much to her, but she sure as hell was going to enjoy it. "This is an important find and I'm proud of the way you persevered. Martin is going to be very grateful for the work you've done, as am I."

"I hope so because my eyes may never be the same," she giggled. "I may be cross-eyed for the rest of my life."

Travis stuck out his lip in mock sympathy. "My poor, poor Aubrey. Is there anything I can do to help ease the...pain?"

It wasn't discomfort that Aubrey was feeling. Far from it, in fact. Her entire body was beginning to hum with pleasure as his large hands ran up and down her back before settling on her bottom, giving the globes a firm squeeze.

Aubrey placed the back of her hand on her forehead and sighed as if she'd just worked a full day in a hot kitchen or maybe ran a marathon. "I'm not sure there's anything anyone can do. I may be beyond all hope."

Smirking and obviously trying not to laugh, Travis slid a hand under her tank top and traced her spine with his fingers. "You do seem to be running a fever. Are you hot?"

You are. Very, very hot.

"It is getting warm in here." Aubrey fanned her face as he lifted her onto his lap. She felt him hard and ready underneath her and she deliberately squirmed, drawing a small groan from his lips. "Maybe I should get undressed."

Travis snapped the lid of the laptop shut and slid it to the floor. "That's a good idea. I also think you need bed rest. Lots of it."

Mmmmm...not alone, I hope.

"Are you hurting anywhere?" Travis asked, his hands gliding over the sensitive flesh of her belly just above the waistband of her sleep shorts. Her panties were already drenched and she had to work to keep her eyelids from drifting shut. His touch was mesmerizing, lulling her into a state where she'd allow him to do just about anything, knowing it would be pure pleasure.

"I hurt everywhere," Aubrey whispered. "But especially here."

Aubrey pointed to her lips.

"And here."

She pointed to her breast. "And here."

Taking a deep breath of courage, she pointed to where her panties were already wet and her clit was tingling.

She must have done something right because Travis was grinning like an idiot, despite her own flush that she could feel from the roots of her hair to the tips of her toes. She'd basically just told him to kiss her intimately and he seemed happy about it.

Aren't I a lucky girl?

"It sounds like you need the full body treatment, Aubrey. Every inch of you needs extra special care. I know just what I need to do. We can't wait a moment more or it might be too late and you'll get worse."

A bar of arousal began to build in her abdomen and white heat swept through her head to toe.

"I do want to feel better," Aubrey cooed, looking up at Travis from under her lashes. "Whatever we need to do I'm fine with. I just have one request."

That dangerous and sexy as hell eyebrow rose. "And that would be?"

"Make me scream, cowboy."

Chapter Twenty-Six

TRAVIS LOVED THIS confident, sexy, and playful side of Aubrey he hadn't been privy to until this weekend. He doubted anyone had and it boosted his ego into the clouds, knowing he'd been a part of this transformation. Now she knew that her past sexual exploits weren't her fault and that she was an amazing, responsive woman.

"By the time we're done here, baby, the guests of this hotel are going to know my damn name because you're going to scream it at the top of your lungs."

It was a promise he intended on keeping. Multiple times.

Aubrey smirked as she ran a fingernail down the middle of his chest. "The Anderson men sure do a lot of bragging."

Someone was in a naughty mood.

"The Anderson men aren't bragging, honey. They're making promises."

She slid up on the bed so her back was against the pillows, a saucy smile playing on her full lips.

"So far I've heard a lot of promises but seen very little action. Is that going to change anytime in the near future?"

That was a challenge if he'd ever heard one. She might as

well have Double Dog dared him to fuck her.

"You don't rush into the full body treatment, young lady. In fact, go take a shower and I'll get things ready out here."

She didn't move a muscle as if she wasn't sure if he was kidding or not. He grabbed her hand and tugged her to her feet before giving her a light swat on her bottom. She squealed and placed her hands back there, rubbing as if to soothe the sting but he knew he hadn't spanked her that hard.

"Move. Take a quick shower and then head back here. Don't bother to put on any clothes as you would only be taking them right off again."

She trembled in his arms but skipped into the bathroom at his bidding. He only had a few minutes but that's all it took to ready the room. First he lowered the lights and drew the curtains for privacy. He tugged the duvet down to the end of the bed so there was plenty of space for the two of them to spread out, then he took Aubrey's vanilla-scented lotion that was currently located on the dresser and placed it on the nightstand. Finally he set his iPod on the clock radio dock and picked a soft, slow, sensual playlist.

The playlist was titled "Relaxing" but tonight it might as well be titled "Songs to Seduce By."

Now that the scene was set, he dashed into the living room relieved to see Shane still sawing logs on the couch. Hopefully he'd sleep through until midday. Travis dug into the refrigerator and pulled out the magnum of champagne he'd asked the management to stock hoping for just this occasion. He tucked the chilled bottle under his arm and snapped up two glass flutes from under the bar before heading back into the bedroom.

The water in the bathroom was off so Aubrey would be joining him any second. He shrugged out of his shirt and jeans so he was only wearing his boxers and then popped open the champagne, pouring the fizzy golden liquid into the glasses just as she opened the bathroom door.

Steam billowed around her head giving her an ethereal appearance, despite being clad in only a thick white towel. She'd clipped up her hair and a few stray strands clung to her damp cheeks. His fingers itched to unclasp the barrette so her chocolate brown hair fell around her shoulders and he could run his fingers through the silky tresses.

"Just how long was I in the shower?"

There was amazement in her tone and he chuckled as he held out the champagne flute. She reached for it and her towel sagged a little, giving it a peek-a-boo effect.

"Long enough. We're going for the whole body treatment here so just lie down on your stomach and relax." She hesitated for a moment and he gave her an encouraging smile. "You trust me, don't you?"

Aubrey took another sip of champagne and then set it on the nightstand next to the vanilla lotion before stretching out on the bed, her head pillowed on her arms. He slid his hands under her and tugged the towel away, leaving her completely bare to his gaze.

Her golden skin beckoned and he squeezed a generous dollop of lotion into his palm, rubbing his hands together to warm it. He gently placed his hands on her shoulders and she jumped slightly at the contact but then let her body go lax, sighing softly as he began to gently knead the muscles.

Travis hummed with pleasure as his fingers traced her womanly curves, skimming the sides of her breasts, down her ribcage, over her hips before gliding back up again. Over and over he repeated his journey until she was putty underneath his palms. His fingers splayed across the small of her back, working the knots he knew were there after hours on the laptop. When he heard her softly moaning he slid his hands down over her heart-shaped ass to massage the muscles of her legs and then finally down to her dainty feet with their cherry-tipped toes.

He pressed his thumbs into her instep and she groaned with pleasure and maybe a little pain as well. While he worked over the soles of her feet he allowed himself the absolute privilege of gazing at her nude form. Her body was an exquisite work of art, made to be worshipped. Others might say her tummy wasn't flat, her breasts too large, or her bottom too round but he thought she was fucking perfect. She looked like a woman, not a stick figure. For a moment he allowed himself to picture what she might look like in a white wedding dress, pregnant with his baby, or even just cuddling with their child reading a story.

Every inch of her was infinitely precious to him and the thought of anything bad happening to her squeezed his chest painfully, making it almost impossible to breathe. In fact, the entire room had to be at least ten degrees hotter than a few minutes ago. He was breathing shallowly and a fine sheen of sweat decorated his skin. If his libido had its way he'd be balls deep within her this very minute. But that wasn't going to happen. Not yet.

She was everything and he'd waited a damn long time to find her. He wouldn't let her go without a fight. Luckily she seemed more than content to make her future with him. He'd even mentioned marriage and she hadn't bolted for the hills as he'd feared.

"Turn over, sweetheart," he said in a voice like gravel, the words sticking in his too tight throat. "Time for your front."

Travis hadn't thought this through.

Aubrey was lying before him like the most sumptuous buffet he could imagine. His erection became painful and his balls drew up closer to his body and he hadn't even been touched yet. This was going to be a long night. Every ounce of blood in his body had rushed to his shaft and now he was gazing at her, probably looking dumbstruck as if he'd never seen a naked woman before.

Snap out of it. Fuck, it's like a furnace in this bedroom.

He gathered more lotion in his palm and ran his hands up and down her legs, her eyes fluttering closed and her lips parted on a sigh of pleasure. He avoided any contact with her most private parts, skipping up to her shoulders and arms but that didn't stop her from writhing under his touch, her hips lifting in invitation. He'd wanted this to go on for much longer but he wasn't sure he could hold back another minute. His mind wasn't working properly and all he could think about was how it was going to feel when she was hot and tight around him, their bodies joined as intimately as possible.

Christ, I'm a mess. Take a deep breath and be patient.

"Travis," Aubrey breathed, her voice a mere wisp of sound that tugged mightily at his heart and farther south as well. "I need you."

"You've got me, baby." He massaged lotion into her full breasts, the nipples tightening under his palms. "Every bit of me."

Plucking at the pale pink tips, he lowered his head and drew one into his mouth before laving it with his tongue, the vanilla scent from her skin wrapping around him. Aubrey hissed with pleasure and her fingernails dug into his shoulders, sending a rocket of pleasure and pain straight to his already aching groin. He was hot, hard, horny as hell, and he only had himself to blame for being frustrated. He'd started this game and he needed to see it through.

After lavishing attention on her nipples he kissed a trail over her belly while he pushed her legs farther apart, situating himself between them. Her fingers curled in his hair, tugging deliciously as he licked up and down her slit, avoiding the one spot she wanted him the most.

Flames coursed through his limbs and settled in his abdomen as his tongue traced patterns around her clit but never giving her the rhythm she needed to go over the cliff. Her legs shook as she pressed her thighs to his head and he dipped two fingers in her tight channel, coming back drenched in her honey.

"Do you want to come, baby? You need to tell me if you do," he cajoled, his fingers slipping deep inside of her and finding that sweet spot that made her wild.

"Yes, yes, yes," she chanted, her head thrown back and her eyes closed in ecstasy. He fucking loved seeing her like this knowing she was feeling the same things he was. Their lovemaking was more than sex. It bonded them together more closely each and every time. "Please, Travis."

"Whatever my lady wants, she gets."

Flattening his tongue, he swiped it back and forth over the

top of her clit before sucking it into his mouth, his teeth lightly scraping the sides. Her response was swift and vocal.

Arching her back, her channel walls tightened on his fingers and a rush of honey drenched his hand. She called out his name over and over as the waves made her body tremble and quake. Travis wasted no time, not letting her come down completely from her high. He ripped off his sweatpants and boxers, impaling her in one deep, soul-destroying thrust.

Groaning, the pleasure rushed from his hard length, down his balls, through his legs, and up his spine. Tight. Hot. Wet. So fucking perfect. He began to move and she rocked her hips in time, her fingers digging into his buttocks.

"Harder. Faster."

He sped up, the sweat pooling at his lower back and his jaw clenched as the pressure built at the base of his spine. Holding back was pure torture but he wanted Aubrey to fly apart one more time before he let himself go. She wrapped her legs around his waist as they set a punishing pace, every stroke rubbing against her already sensitized clit. He felt her clench around him and knew she was almost there.

"Come for me. Let go, I've got you."

And you've got me.

He was relentless, pistoning in and out of her like a metronome, the sweat pouring off of him and the pressure in his balls turning to excruciating agony. He thought he might burst a blood vessel but then her walls fluttered and clenched, her back arching and his name on her lips.

Her climax wrung his own from him, black spots dotted his vision and it felt like he was being turned inside out as his seed shot from his balls and deep inside of his most perfect woman. He groaned a few words that he couldn't even understand and collapsed on top of her, his breath coming in ragged chunks as he sucked air into his starved lungs. Her fingers trailed up and down his damp spine and he heard her sigh of satisfaction. They stayed just like that as the world ceased to spin around them, time having no meaning as their lips met one more time in a kiss of love and tenderness.

When some blood had returned to his brain he realized he was crushing the woman he loved to death and he rolled over on his back, his arm around her pulling her close so he wouldn't miss a moment of feeling her skin next to his.

She laid her cheek on his chest and traced patterns on his belly. "I can hear your heart racing."

What they had just shared was too monumental. He couldn't keep the words inside any longer.

"It doesn't belong to me anymore. It's your heart now."

Travis could feel Aubrey hold her breath and he could swear that same heart in question stopped beating for a moment as he waited for her response. When he didn't get one, he knew he'd fucked up.

It was too soon.

He'd pushed too hard.

She just didn't love him.

Then she sat up and looked him right in the eye, a few shimmery silver tears sliding down her cheeks.

"I'll take good care of it. I promise. I love you, Travis."

Her voice was shaky but she never looked away, not trying to hide her crying. This wasn't the moment to try and be cool. He was as overcome with emotion, if not more. His mouth and tongue didn't seem to be working very well and it took him a few tries before he was able to form actual words.

"I love you too. So very much."

They cuddled together, pressed close from head to toe. No more words needed to be said. They'd crossed a milestone and everything at that moment became better. It became more.

He would spend the rest of his life loving, adoring, and protecting Aubrey Grayson.

Chapter Twenty-Seven

AUBREY, TRAVIS, AND Shane were having breakfast down-stairs in the hotel dining room the next morning and she and Travis kept sneaking looks at each other and smiling while holding hands under the table. Apparently they hadn't been all that inconspicuous though, because finally Shane slapped his fork down with a mock sigh of frustration.

"I can just find a table by myself if you'd like me gone. I feel like the proverbial fifth wheel. I can only imagine what happened between you two after I fell asleep." Shane held up his hands with a grin. "And I sure as hell don't want to know either. But both of you have been giving each other sly smiles since I opened my eyes this morning. I'm happy for you and all, but please don't offend my delicate sensibilities and start going at it right here on the table. I'm way too innocent for that."

Feeling the heat rise in her cheeks, Aubrey couldn't contain her nervous giggle. "Innocent? You? I have never heard anyone describe you that way, Shane Anderson. Not one. In fact, I heard a story about you, Sissie Mae Watkins, and a hay loft that just about curled my hair. Is it true?"

Travis chuckled over his coffee cup and nodded, not giving

his cousin a chance to answer. "Shane can't even see innocent in the rearview mirror—that's how far he is from it. And yes, that story is true. Every damn word. Hell, there are probably parts we haven't even heard about that would scar us for life."

Shane groaned and signaled to the waitress for a coffee refill. "I don't have to take this abuse."

"Yes, you do," Travis laughed. "You earned every bit of it. Admit it, you enjoy your debauched life."

A grin spread across Shane's handsome face. All the Anderson men were too gorgeous for their own good. "Every single second of it, and Sissie Mae is a particularly pleasant memory, if I may say so. That was a good night."

The waitress refilled their coffees but Travis barely noticed. He appeared to be enjoying this trip down memory lane. "You almost burned the Watkins's barn down. I think her daddy still has a restraining order on you."

"You worry too much," Shane scoffed as his phone began to chime. "It was just a little harmless fun and no one got hurt. Seriously, anyway. Excuse me, I need to take this."

He swiped the screen and stepped away from the table to the outdoor patio, the day already sunny and warm, leaving Aubrey and Travis alone at the table.

"He's right, you know. I can't take my eyes off of you. You look even more beautiful than usual this morning." Travis lifted her hand and brushed his lips across her knuckles and then her fingertips, his gaze taking in the simple white sundress she'd chosen to wear today. "I love you."

Her throat tightened up and her breath quickened. Would he always have this potent of an effect on her? "I love you too. A lot."

"Good, because that's how I feel too." He leaned closer and she could smell his fresh from the shower scent, yummy enough to make her want to abandon her breakfast and drag him upstairs, stripping the conservative khaki pants and shirt from his delectable body. "What would you say if I planned a vacation for us? Just you and me. No work and no interruptions."

"I thought this was supposed to be a vacation."

Travis grimaced as his gaze strayed to where Shane was standing outside the windows of the restaurant. "It certainly hasn't turned out to be much of one. I want us to have a real vacation. How about I rent one of those beach houses and we go somewhere that doesn't have Wi-Fi?"

He was dreaming and Aubrey knew it better than anyone. "I keep your schedule, remember? When do you think we'll find this magic time in your calendar? You're booked for the next six months or more. The only reason we were able to come here is because you can work from the suite." She patted his hand comfortingly. "It's okay. I know that you're an incredibly busy man. I've told you before but I'll say it again. I don't need you to cater to me, Travis. I'm independent and can take care of myself."

Instead of being happy or relieved he was actually scowling at her words. "I wouldn't mind it if you needed me just a little bit. I like taking care of you."

"I do need you." Aubrey tried to put as much feeling into her words as possible, wanting Travis to understand. "I need you to love me. I need you in my life because I love having you there. But I don't need you to pay my bills or make everything in my life perfect. That's not your job. I wouldn't be much of a partner if I didn't row the boat with you."

"What if you get tired of rowing?"

"What if you do?" she shot back. "Your needs are just as important as mine."

She stopped there, letting her words sink into the hard head of the stubborn as hell man she loved more than anything in the world. His sense of honor was one of the reasons she admired him so much but it was going to be the death of her. She wanted a man by her side, not a father looking over her shoulder.

Their conversation wouldn't be finished however as Shane joined them again, slapping his phone down on the table. "That was an interesting conversation."

"Are you going to share with the class?" Travis asked, sitting back in his chair. He looked relaxed but Aubrey could see the tension that had crept into his frame. He was taking this entire murder case onto his own shoulders, wanting to clear Martin's name.

"As a matter of fact, I am." Shane leaned forward, his gaze circling the dining room and then coming back to rest on Aubrey and Travis. "That was the reporter contact I made at the local newspaper. He told me a few fascinating things, first and foremost that although it's only a preliminary report, the coroner is leaning toward ruling Iris's death an accident."

Aubrey's jaw fell open. "An accident? How can that be?"

"According to the reporter, her blood alcohol level was twice the legal limit which means she was probably feeling no pain when she went into the water. In her room was an almost empty champagne bottle so it looks like she drank the whole thing.

Their theory is she got drunk because she was upset about Bruce's death, took a walk outside maybe to get some air, then fell in the pool and was so incapacitated she couldn't get out."

Travis rubbed his chin, obviously not convinced. "This looks fishy to me. First, we're to believe that she was depressed, which when you and Aubrey talked to her she clearly was not. Then I have to buy into the fact that she drank an entire bottle of champagne. By herself. Don't people drink champagne to celebrate things? And then she wandered outside to the pool, fell in, and drowned. I'm not feeling this."

Iris hadn't seemed like a depressed drinker but then Aubrey had only spoken to her that one time.

"Maybe she finally accepted that Bruce was gone," she suggested. "And when it hit her she just couldn't take the pain."

"Both explanations are plausible," Shane shrugged. "They're also running a tox screen on Iris's blood but they won't get that back for days. What's important here is that the reporter talked to Detective Prather this morning after he saw the preliminary report and the detective believes there is no connection between the two deaths."

"In other words, Martin is still on the hook," Travis finished for him. "I was hoping that there would be some evidence linking Bruce and Iris together that would exonerate Martin. I sent the photo Aubrey found to his attorney this morning but I'm not sure if that's going to help him get bail. The judge has been quite uncooperative."

"This is a murder case," Aubrey reminded him gently. "Plus Martin has vast resources. They consider him a flight risk."

Shane tapped the table with his phone. "There's more."

"Of course there is," Travis sighed. "More good news I assume?"

"The final autopsy report for Bruce was filed. It appears that he had sleeping pills in his system. A lot of them. That would have made him sleepy and possibly easy to handle when he was lured out to the beach."

"So a woman could have done it," Aubrey murmured, thinking about Iris's untimely demise. "Do you think Iris did it and then out of guilt offed herself?"

Travis scraped a hand down his face, his expression a mask of tension. "That is entirely possible. From what we know she and Bruce were seeing each other but perhaps she was pushing him for more. Maybe she wanted him to leave Caroline and he refused."

Shane leveled a gaze at Travis. "But you still don't believe it was an accident, do you?"

"No," Travis finally replied, clearly not happy about admitting it. "No, I don't. I'm sorry but it's too much of a coincidence. I think Iris's death was probably not accidental and I think it has something to do with Bruce's. But I can't prove any of it."

Pursing his lips, Shane drummed his fingers against his coffee cup. "We've gone over the suspects but what about the evidence? How about the cufflink? If Martin didn't accidentally drop it stabbing Bruce in the heart then it was planted there. Who might have access to those cufflinks?"

Travis tapped his chin in thought. "Alana. Caroline. The housekeeping staff, but we have to assume they have no motive to frame Martin. Caroline has the most motive of course."

It appeared Travis didn't enjoy admitting that either.

"Certainly a wife might want her husband and his girlfriend dead but what does she gain?" Aubrey queried. "In Caroline's case she wouldn't have gained anything except her freedom and she could have gotten that with a divorce."

Shane snapped his fingers. "Money? Did she have a prenup with Bruce? If not, she might have been on the hook for a big chunk of change."

Travis sighed and shook his head. "They had one. Martin made sure of it. Ironclad too from what he said. If Bruce and Caroline divorced he came out with a small settlement of two hundred and fifty thousand. Hardly the millions he'd grown accustomed to."

"Then Caroline wouldn't have much to gain by killing Bruce and Iris," Aubrey pointed out. "Except for revenge. Honestly she didn't look like the vengeful type. She seems really sweet."

"She is," Travis agreed with a small smile. "But she's also been the type to not stand up for herself, which is exactly how she ended up in a rotten marriage with Bruce. Any other woman would have kicked him to the curb a long time ago."

Shane drained his coffee cup and signaled to the waitress for the check. "Then I think we know what we need to do."

Aubrey's brows shot up. "We do?"

"We do," Travis confirmed. "We need to talk to Caroline and Alana. They had access to the cufflinks."

Shane signed for the bill and the three of them stood, exiting the restaurant.

"So how do we do this? Good cop, bad cop?" Aubrey asked. How did one ask if their friend had a motive for murder? She wasn't that good at all this cloak and dagger business.

Travis rubbed the back of his neck. "We're their friends and we're trying to help."

Aubrey rolled her eyes and followed Travis and Shane into the elevator. "If they're innocent and our friends this should go great. If one of them is the killer this could get kind of ugly."

The kind of ugly that could get dangerous.

Chapter Twenty-Eight

I T WAS DECIDED that Shane and Aubrey would go back to the suite and that Travis would talk to Caroline and Alana since he knew them the best. Travis knocked on Martin's hotel room door and was surprised when Tom Lovell was the one who opened it.

"Tom," Travis greeted the younger man. "I'm here to see Caroline and Alana."

He waited for Tom to step aside but instead he stood in the doorway. "Alana's not here. She's down in the spa trying to relax. She was very upset when the judge wouldn't give Martin bail."

Interesting way to deal with it. A mani-pedi or maybe a facial.

"Then I'd like to see Caroline, please."

Travis kept his voice level, showing no aggression but also no surrender. The two men stared each other down for a few moments but then a voice from inside the suite shattered the tension.

"Tom? Who's at the door?"

Caroline.

"It's Travis. I told him this isn't a good time."

"No, I want to see him." Caroline squeezed next to Tom, frowning at his recalcitrant attitude. "Let him in for Pete's sake. He's a friend."

Travis heartily hoped she believed that thirty minutes from now.

"Would you like some coffee, Travis? Or maybe a soft drink?"

"No, thank you." Travis sat on the couch and Caroline settled in a chair next to it. Tom didn't sit, choosing instead to hover in the background as if ready to pounce at a moment's notice.

"I want to thank you so much for finding that photograph of Granddad wearing the other set of cufflinks." Caroline sighed and curled into the cushions, a mug held in her hands. "The attorney is having another go at the judge that denied bail. He seems optimistic that it might help if it raises doubts as to his guilt."

"It was actually Aubrey who found it but I'm glad that we could help in some small way. How are you holding up with all this?"

Caroline's teeth sunk into her lower lip before answering. "I'm just trying to take everything moment to moment and day by day. I'm not thinking about the future right now. I hate the fact that Granddad is in jail. I know he didn't do this. He hated Bruce but he wouldn't kill anyone."

Travis didn't beat around the bush. "If Martin was wearing different cufflinks than what they found underneath the body that means they were planted by the killer. Do you know who might have had access to the suite and to Martin's belongings?"

Caroline's nail tapped the ceramic mug. "Me. Alana. Bruce. Housekeeping, of course. I think that's it."

"So you and Bruce were staying in the suite with Martin and Alana?"

"Yes, not that Bruce was here all that often." Tears shimmered in the young woman's eyes but her chin was bravely lifted. "He spent a great deal of time...out."

"Out?" Travis echoed, not wanting to push but needing to know if there was someone else that they didn't know about. "Was he conducting business over the weekend?"

Tom stopped pacing and stared down at Travis with disgust. "Christ, we all know what Bruce was doing. He was with his slut Iris Perry."

Caroline winced at the blunt statement but then nodded her head, a sad expression on her face.

"Tom's right. Bruce spent most of his time with Iris, and honestly our marriage was to the point that I was glad that he did. He never missed an opportunity to tell me what a disappointment of a wife I was and being with him had become increasingly difficult. We've basically been living apart for the last six months."

"You should have left him a long time ago," Tom muttered, restarting his pacing.

"I should have," Caroline agreed. "But I didn't. He had me convinced our problems were all my fault and if I just changed everything would be better. I finally realized that nothing was ever going to make our relationship a good one. I'd screwed up picking a husband and I guess I thought that I had to suffer for my mistake. That this was my punishment."

"You were young and you made an error in judgment. Suffering the rest of your life for it seems like overkill," Travis argued. "Especially when he was cheating on you."

"I'm not sorry he's dead," Caroline whispered, her voice tortured and low. "He used to yell at me, calling me names. Sometimes he'd physically intimidate me by backing me into a corner and then screaming at me. He made me feel like nothing. Now that he's gone I'm finally free."

Jesus, Mary, and Joseph. The poor girl.

Bruce was worse than Travis had thought and that was pretty damn bad.

Tom rounded the couch and sat on the arm of Caroline's chair, placing a comforting hand on her shoulder. "It's okay, Caro. You don't have to talk about this."

The man gave Travis a glare of dislike as tears began to slide down Caroline's cheeks. Travis didn't feel good about this line of questioning but the police would be much less gentle.

"I'm sorry. I didn't mean to upset you."

The door flew open and Alana breezed in, a smile on her face until she took in the scene before her – Caroline crying, Tom comforting, and Travis sitting there uncomfortable and grim. She dropped her purse on the floor and held out her arms to the distraught young woman.

"Sweetheart, what's the matter? Come here, honey. Let me give you a big hug." Alana jerked her head toward the bar. "Tom, get Caro a drink. A strong one."

"It's ten in the morning," Tom protested but did as the older woman asked after she gave him a quelling look. "I guess one wouldn't hurt."

"I'm sorry I've upset you–" Travis began but Caroline held up her hand and shook her head.

"I've been upset for a long time, honestly. I'll admit the events of the last week haven't helped but these tears aren't about you. They're about my life and what a mess I've made of it."

"Honey, you're going to be fine." Alana perched on the edge of the chair and wrapped her arms around the young woman. "The world will always try and bitch slap you but you just have to get up and kick them in the balls right back. Don't let anyone tell you to lie down and take their crap."

Travis crossed his legs, uncomfortable with the thought of anyone getting kicked in the privates no matter what they'd done. Tom was shifting on his feet as well as if he wasn't happy about the imagery either. He finished mixing some champagne and orange juice in a flute and came to sit down on Caroline's other side, handing her the drink.

She made a face but Alana tapped the glass and gave Caroline a stern look. "Drink. It will relax you. You've been living on caffeine for the last several days so this isn't any worse."

Travis narrowed his eyes as he took in Tom's worried countenance and the way the man's hand patted Caroline's knee. Travis had always assumed that Tom was Bruce's friend but perhaps he was more Caroline's friend.

"Are you going to see Martin today?" Travis decided changing the topic of conversation would be a good idea.

Alana dragged a decorative throw off the back of the sofa and tucked it around Caroline despite the temperature outside of near eighty degrees. He was impressed by the woman's motherly instincts even if he wasn't as impressed by her devotion as a wife.

"Yes, Tom is going to drive me there this morning."

"I want to go too," Caroline pushed down the cashmere fabric so it was around her waist instead of her neck. "I need to see that Granddad is okay."

Tom and Alana were already shaking their heads before Caroline even finished talking.

"You need to rest," Tom replied, another pat to her hand. "Going to the county jail is only going to upset you."

"I'm a grown woman and it won't hurt me to be upset. Not being upset that my grandfather is in jail for murdering my husband would be much worse, don't you think?"

"Your grandfather is a strong man and he will be fine in any situation." Alana dug into her purse and pulled out her phone to check her messages. "I agree with Tom on this. You should stay here and rest."

The scene was rather surreal. Alana and Tom were treating Caroline like she didn't have a brain in her head. The look on the young woman's face told the story as well. She was tired of it and was about to say something scathing. Perhaps Travis could do something to alleviate the growing tension between the three.

"Caroline, how about you and Aubrey go downstairs to the spa and have a nice relaxing massage? Aubrey has been saying she's wanted to go but I haven't had the time to go with her. She'd love the company."

Alana clapped her hands together and smiled. "That sounds like a wonderful idea. Some girl time never hurts."

Caroline opened her mouth to object but Travis tried his best to give her a side eye that silently told her to trust him.

Instead she acquiesced, her gaze still on Travis. "I guess I could do that. I really liked talking with Aubrey the other day. She and I got along really well. And I'd like a chance to thank her as well for finding the photo."

Travis stood and gave Caroline a meaningful look. "Why don't you come to our suite when you're ready? In the meantime I'll call down to the spa and make the arrangements."

Nodding, Caroline's gaze rocketed between him, Tom, and Alana before finally settling back on Travis. "I just need to freshen up a little."

"No hurry. We'll be waiting. Tom. Alana. Nice to see you. Tell Martin we're thinking about him."

"Of course we will, Travis. I know my husband is grateful for everything you've done." Alana opened the door for him and he had a feeling she was glad to see him go.

"Call me if you need anything."

Travis had a feeling that call was never going to come.

As he walked down the hall to the elevator he couldn't help but think there was something very strange about the dynamics of those three people. He couldn't quite put his finger on it, but in his gut he knew there was something that wasn't right.

He just needed to figure out what it was.

Chapter Twenty-Nine

AUBREY AND CAROLINE were down in the spa so that left Travis and Shane to try and find out more about the relationship between Caroline, Alana, and Tom. Travis only had one word for it.

Dysfunctional.

There had clearly been an undercurrent of some kind of history between them and knowing about it might give Travis some insight into Bruce's murder. He and Shane were in the elevator hoping to catch the resort maid that serviced Tom's room. Travis wanted to know if Caroline had been seen anywhere in the vicinity. He didn't want to believe that she was someone capable of murder but he'd ignored her motive for far too long.

"You're pissed."

Shane certainly had a way of summing up fucked up situations. But he was wrong. Travis wasn't pissed off, he was livid.

"Yes, and your point is?"

Shane reached around Travis and slapped the emergency stop button on the elevator and the car came to a shuddering halt.

"My point is you better pull your shit together and fast. I get that you wanted to clear Aubrey's name because you're in love with her and now you want to clear Martin because he's been like a second father, but you're letting this case get to you. Ultimately it is not your job to find this killer. It's Prather's job and while he might not be doing everything you want, he is investigating from what that reporter told me. You just don't like what he's found."

Anger and frustration churned in Travis's gut. He'd never felt so helpless in his life.

"It's a good thing it's not my job because I'm piss poor at it. If it had been Aubrey would be on death row about now."

"Is that why you've got your knickers in a twist? Because you're not good at catching criminals? You know that's not your real job, right? You're a businessman and a damn good one but honestly, Travis, you're an amateur detective and no, it doesn't make any difference that two of your brothers are cops. If they were musicians would you book a concert hall for yourself and sell tickets? Give yourself a fucking break."

Travis's jaw tightened and he had to swallow a not so pleasant retort. Shane didn't understand.

"Fine, consider me lectured," Travis growled. "Can we go now?"

Shane insinuated himself between Travis and the elevator button. "No. In fact, hell no. We are not done here. You're still being a dick and not listening to me. You're doing the best you can. That's all you and I can do. The fact you need to face is that Martin just might be guilty. That's the eight-hundred pound elephant in the room you're ignoring."

Travis slumped back against the elevator wall with a groan.

"I just can't believe that. Not Martin."

"I don't want to believe it either. I like Martin. He seems like a good guy but I've always believed that anyone is capable of murder if motivated enough. If a mother was protecting her child, you would think she could kill. So if Martin were protecting Caroline he might kill Bruce. All I'm saying is that it is possible and we can't pretend it's not true."

Rubbing the back of his neck, Travis nodded in defeat. He couldn't fight this much longer and it was making everything more difficult than it needed to be. "Fine. Martin might have done it. He's capable of it. But so are a lot of people."

Shane pushed the red button and the elevator lurched as it began its descent once again. "Luckily we aren't looking at a lot of people. We're only looking at a few. Right now we want to find out if Tom and Caroline have some sort of relationship that we don't know about. Something more than friends. Then we can go back and talk about Martin as a possibility."

The doors slid open and Travis and Shane exited the elevator heading straight down the hall to where a housekeeper and her cart full of supplies was working her way through the rooms. Stepping back, Travis let Shane take the lead on talking to the woman. His cousin could charm the birds from the trees and definitely had some sort of voodoo when it came to females. He was their best chance of learning anything.

"Good afternoon, ma'am." Shane gave the older woman a wide smile. "My name is Shane and this is my cousin Travis. We were hoping you could perhaps help us? It would only take a moment."

The woman lifted an armful of towels from the cart but

didn't go into the room she was cleaning, which wasn't a surprise. The service in the resort was exemplary and she was certainly in the habit of helping a lost or confused guest.

"How can I help you, sir?"

Shane chuckled as he leaned casually against the cart. "Please call me Shane. I won't take up much of your time as I'm sure you're very busy." Looking down at the floor, somehow Travis's cousin managed to blush slightly. "I'm a little embarrassed to admit this but I'm looking for a woman. One woman in particular and I was wondering if you'd seen her around. I think the man in this room is her brother."

Shane pulled one of the photos from the party from his shirt pocket and handed it to the housekeeper, pointing to Caroline. "Have you seen the pretty blonde around here? I danced with her once and I simply cannot get her out of my mind. I think I might be in love."

Travis had to hide his smile at how Shane sighed like a sad Romeo looking for his Juliet. But it explained his amazing success picking up women.

The housekeeper chuckled and took the picture from Shane, examining it closely, before shaking her head. "I've never seen her before but she's pretty."

Shane's gaze shifted to Travis then back to the woman. "Are you sure? You've never seen her around here?"

The housekeeper tapped the photo. "No, I'd remember someone like her. I'm sorry I can't help you."

It still left the question as to what the undercurrent was between Caroline, Tom, and Alana but perhaps it didn't have a thing to do with Bruce's death.

"I appreciate that you tried to help." Shane gave her his best smile. "I'm sorry I didn't catch your name, darlin'."

"Charlotte," she offered. "My friends call me Lotte."

"That's a beautiful name for a beautiful lady." Shane tucked the photograph back into his pocket. "Thank you so much for helping me. I hope you won't mention this to anyone. I'm rather embarrassed about being so smitten with a woman I only danced with once."

"It's like Cinderella," Lotte declared with a laugh. "And you're her Prince Charming."

Hiding his laugh with a cough, Travis nodded in agreement. "It is romantic, isn't it? You just don't see men going all out to find the woman of their dreams these days."

"No, you don't," Lotte agreed with a harrumph. "Men and women seemed to have lost the romance from life. They're all too busy staring at their phones."

"Well, I do thank you again for your help. I just know I'm going to find her."

"Good luck. I hope you do."

Lotte waved as she disappeared into the hotel room with a stack of towels. Shane and Travis hightailed it back to the elevator, not saying a word until the doors quietly slid closed.

Another dead end.

✦ ✦ ✦

TRAVIS, AUBREY, SHANE, and Caroline were sitting in the dining room the next morning eating breakfast and filling in a few stray details from the case. A few gently probing questions to the delicate blonde revealed that she had known Tom Lovell for several years. She'd met him when she'd started dating Bruce and she'd always found him to be a good, loyal friend even when Bruce didn't deserve it.

Travis had managed to get Caroline in to see Martin the day before after Alana had left the county jail. She reported back that her grandfather was in good spirits but he looked tired and thin. The attorney had another meeting with the judge today so hopefully this time bail would be set and they could get Martin free.

"What do you ladies have planned today?" Shane asked, popping a home fry into his mouth. "Going to see Martin again?"

Aubrey and Caroline were becoming fast friends and were already talking about meeting up with Brinley and Gigi when Caroline joined them in Tremont. It was good to see Aubrey making friends so easily. From what she'd told him, she had a hard time when she was in school with the other snotty girls being so mean to her. Now she knew she had nothing to be ashamed of and with any luck it would bring her out of her shell. She'd been alone too long.

"The resort rents out bicycles so Caro and I thought we'd take a ride up the beach. It's supposed to be a gorgeous day." Aubrey and Caroline were all smiles, both dressed casually in shorts and cotton t-shirts, tennis shoes on their feet. "Are you boys interested in coming with us?"

The case was at a standstill. Travis and Shane didn't have any new information to go on and it was frustrating as hell. It seemed that the cufflink photo might be the only thing they could do to help Martin. West and Jason were always saying that criminals weren't very smart but it appeared that this one at least might have pulled off the perfect crime.

In fact, it might be time for Travis, Aubrey, and Shane to return to Montana. He was able to do most of the work that needed to be done from here along with Aubrey's help, but there were some things he needed to be at the office for. If he couldn't help Martin he might as well go somewhere where he was needed. He'd talk to Aubrey about leaving in the morning.

"Why not? It's a nice day as you said so we might as well get outside and enjoy it."

They were finishing up breakfast when Tom strode into the dining room and right up to their table. He was dressed as informally as the rest of them but the hard set of his jaw looked to be anything but relaxed.

"I've been looking for you everywhere, Caro."

The strange dynamics at work again. To her credit, Caroline didn't bark back at him that her whereabouts weren't any of his business. She composed her features into a sweet smile and dabbed at her lips with the napkin.

"I've been here for the last hour so I'm not sure what the mystery is. What's going on?"

Clearly annoyed, Tom exhaled noisily, his nostrils flaring. "Alana needs to talk to you. The police have been up in your suite questioning her about the cufflinks."

The dining room overlooked the lobby but Prather must have come in the back door to avoid the press that had started to camp out in front of the building since Iris's death. Even if Prather didn't think there was a connection, the reporters had different hopes. They had to sell papers and a double murder would ensure that.

Caroline's eyes widened at the news and she tossed her napkin aside, beginning to lever up from the chair. "I better get up there."

Shane put his hand on her shoulder and pressed her back down. "No need. It looks like the detective is coming to you. I'll stay right here with you. You shouldn't answer any questions without a lawyer present."

"I don't really have one so thank you. I guess I could call Granddad's attorney. He was with me the last time."

"That's not a good idea. It would be a conflict of interest for him to represent both of you," Travis warned. "It's best to have your own lawyer. Shane can fill that role until you find a local person."

Detective Prather was flanked by two other men both in plainclothes which made Travis feel slightly better. If they were there to arrest Alana or Caroline uniformed cops probably would also have made the trip. Their absence was a positive sign.

"Good morning, Mrs. Livingston." The detective nodded at the group. "I was hoping you could come to the station for a few questions we need answered."

Shane didn't let Caroline answer, squeezing her hand reassuringly. "Why can't we do this here?"

"I'd feel more comfortable at the station." The gleam in the detective's eye told a different story. This new wrinkle wasn't anything good.

"I'm accompanying Mrs. Livingston as her counsel," stated Shane, standing so he was eye to eye with Prather. "Unless you are charging her I reserve the right to call a halt to your questioning at any time."

"Of course," Prather answered smoothly. "It's just a few questions that came up after talking to Mrs. Guinness."

Tom's face had grown darker with every passing moment, muttering under his breath. "I'm coming along as well."

"I'm fine." Caroline shook her head. "Shane will be there. You should go up and be with Alana. I'm sure she's very upset."

"I'm more worried about you," he argued, a muscle flexing in his jaw. "You shouldn't be alone."

"I'm not alone. Please go up and check on Alana." Caroline didn't budge and finally Tom spun on his heel, a few choice words on his lips, and stalked to the elevator. "I'm ready to go, Detective."

"We'll follow you in our car back to the station." Shane placed his hand on Caroline's arm to guide her but it was probably more for moral support. "After you, Caro."

Detective Prather and his men filed out of the dining room toward the back entrance.

Were they building a new case against Caroline or was this questioning to bolster the evidence they thought they already had against Martin? And what had Alana told them that made them want to question Caroline? At the station, no less.

Prather had to know something that they didn't, which had Travis catching up to Shane before they could exit the resort.

"I need the name of that reporter you've been talking to. I think we need to know *everything* he knows."

West's words echoed in Travis's brain, over and over again.

Don't worry about the motives. Look at the evidence.

He wouldn't have a moment's peace until he heeded his

brother's words. He thought he had been but he could see clearly now that he'd been caught up following the police's investigation rather than leading his own. Prather was looking at motives, concentrating his efforts there. Travis needed to look at the places and people that the detective was ignoring.

That's where the truth would lie.

Chapter Thirty

THE QUESTIONING OF Caroline had gone on for over two hours but Detective Prather had finally let her come back to the resort with Shane. Aubrey was proud of the way Caroline had held her own, not letting the cop shake her. One thing was clear, there was no way Caroline was guilty of killing her husband. Aubrey had been in foster care and she'd met evil people and this young woman didn't even come close.

The two of them had decided to spend the rest of the day in Caroline's suite watching pay-per-view movies and ordering room service. Caroline deserved it after the crappy morning she'd had and Aubrey had promised to indulge her brand new friend with anything that would get her mind off of all that had happened in the last week.

"We can order pizza and chocolate cake and eat it while we watch chick flicks," Aubrey declared as Caroline slid the key card into the suite door lock. "I think the guys are a little jealous. Not of the movies but of the junk food. Travis has quite the sweet tooth."

"You're so lucky to have someone like him. I'd love to be adored like that."

The lock clicked and they crossed into the living room, the blast of cold from the air conditioning chilling their skin. This suite looked very much like their own although the furnishings were a different style, more traditional with darker wood and fabrics.

Caroline headed straight for the phone on the coffee table. "I'll order the food and you can pick out a movie."

Aubrey had already taken a few steps toward the oversized flatscreen on the wall when she saw a movement out of the corner of her eye. Caroline had received a text from Alana saying she was having drinks with a few friends but apparently she was still in the suite. Although Aubrey was admittedly uncomfortable around the older woman she was still Martin's wife and it would be rude to exclude her from the planned festivities.

"Alana," she called, walking over to the door to the bedroom but hesitating just outside. The door was half open and she could hear movement within the room. "Caroline and I are going to order some food and watch a movie. Do you want to join us?"

No answer.

Caroline was holding the phone in her hand, a confused expression on her face. "Alana is downstairs in the bar having drinks."

"No, she's here."

Caroline laughed and hung up the phone, breezing past Aubrey and pushing open the bedroom door. "Alana, did you change your mind? We're having a girl's afternoon and you can join us."

Aubrey's heart stuttered and her stomach clenched. Standing

before them was Tom Lovell with a knife in one hand and a prescription pill bottle in the other.

His mouth was hanging open and his skin had gone pale.

Then just as quickly he recovered his charm, smiling casually as if there was nothing strange about him standing in Martin and Alana's bedroom holding cutlery with a handkerchief.

"Caroline, I thought you were still at the station."

The young women blinked once, and then twice. "They let me come home. Shane called a halt to the questioning and they didn't charge me with anything." She moved farther into the room. "What are you doing in here, Tom?"

He shoved his hands, and everything in them, in his blazer pockets and chuckled. "Alana asked me to get her a few things, that's all."

Aubrey's gaze darted back and forth between Caroline and Tom as the tension in the room ratcheted up uncomfortably. Despite the cool temperature, sweat had popped out on Tom's forehead and was trickling down his temple and into his dark hair.

"I don't think Alana would do that." Caroline was shaking her head slowly, her shoulders tense. "I think you need to leave."

"Sure she did. She wanted me to grab a sweater for her. The dining room is cold."

Still the charming smile but Tom's lower lip trembled slightly at the corner. Aubrey remembered that same "tell" on Alan Morton but at the time she hadn't known what it meant. Then he'd kidnapped her and Gigi and tried to kill them.

How did she manage to get herself into these situations?

Swallowing down a lump of fear that had risen in her throat,

Aubrey grabbed Caroline's arm and cautiously took a step back. "You know, we should take that sweater down to Alana and join her for that drink. It'll be fun."

Luckily Caroline seemed as creeped out as Aubrey. She too moved back toward the door but kept her gaze on the man standing next to the dresser. "I could really use a drink. Yes, let's go join Alana and the boys. Why don't you send them a text and tell them to meet us downstairs instead of coming up here?"

"Good idea." Aubrey cautiously reached for the zipper on her purse, nerves making the skin on her back damp, her t-shirt sticking to the flesh. "We can always sit out by the pool or something."

Caroline turned around to make a hasty exit, Aubrey right on her heels, still fumbling with her handbag. Aubrey was breathing easier when they made it all the way out of the bedroom and were only a few feet from the door but then she heard Tom's voice.

"You need to stop. Drop your purses on the floor and kick them back here." Aubrey's breath hissed out and she closed her eyes for a moment as her heart pounded against her ribcage. She was fucked. Again. "Turn around. Slowly."

Handbags thudded to the floor while the two women reluctantly, glacially, turned back.

It was then that Aubrey saw what deep shit she and Caroline were in. The dangerous and deadly kind.

Tom had a gun pointed at them, his face gray and his eyes glassy and dead.

They'd be lucky to get out of this alive.

✦   ✦   ✦

SHANE AND TRAVIS sat at the dining table in the suite, papers spread all over the surface. Shane had once again contacted the reporter and after promising unprecedented access to the Anderson family personally in addition to Anderson Industries, they now had copies of every piece of paper that the reporter had including coroner reports, forensics, and statements made to the police.

Travis held up one of the files, pulling Shane from what he was studying. "This is interesting. These are the statements from the guests at the party. Aubrey and I were dancing at the time of the murder. Caroline was at the bar talking with an old friend of the family. Alana and Tom were sitting outside on the patio chatting and Iris said she went upstairs to her room to change her stockings because one had a run. A waitress said that she saw Iris heading for the elevators."

Shane shrugged. "So everyone is accounted for. That's nothing new."

"The elevators are on the way to the back exit which would take her to the beach."

Frowning, Shane rubbed his chin in thought. "Okay. So you're going with the police theory that Iris killed Bruce and then got upset about it and accidentally drowned."

Travis flipped open the file and tapped on one of the papers. "Stay with me here. That's not what I'm thinking at all. Look at Alana and Tom's statements. They alibi each other. Don't you think that's strange? They're off on the patio, no one else sees them, and only they can vouch for each other."

Shane stood and walked over to the windows overlooking the Gulf, stretching his arms over his head after being seated for so long. "That is weird. But it's not evidence that they committed a crime and then helped each other cover it up."

Travis sat back in the chair, remembering back to that morning when they'd visited Martin's suite after Bruce had been killed. "Bruce had sleeping pills in his system and Alana takes sleeping pills. She admitted it the day after."

"You think Alana and Tom are working together? For what purpose? Why kill Bruce? And maybe Iris? What's the end game?"

Scraping his fingers through his hair, Travis groaned in frustration. "I don't fucking know. Why kill Bruce? What does anyone gain from it? He didn't have any money to inherit. He was cheating on his wife but how would that affect Tom and Alana?"

Shane picked up a watered down glass of soda and drank what was left. "Well, whoever did this managed to disrupt many lives while they were at it. You, me, and Aubrey have stayed extra days. Caroline now faces widowhood. And Martin is sitting in the county jail."

And so far Travis hadn't been able to do much about that last item.

"So many unintended consequences–" Travis began but then stopped, an idea slamming him straight between the eyes.

Unintended.

I've been thinking about this all fucking wrong.

"You've got that 'I bought a stock and it just went up four hundred percent' look. Want to share what's going on in that brain of yours?" Shane asked, his brows shooting up almost to his hairline. "You're scaring me honestly with the look on your face. I think you had that same expression when West accidentally hit you with a two by two when you were both cleaning out the horse barn. Stunned, I believe is what your mom called it."

Travis sprang to his feet, a grin spreading across his face. "We've been assuming all this time that these were *unintended* consequences. But what if they were completely intended? Planned, in fact?"

"You think someone planned that Caroline be a widow and that Martin is in jail? Why? Who benefits?"

Leaning back against the windows, Travis tapped his chin, his thoughts going a mile a minute. Finally it felt like he was making progress after days of standing in quicksand.

"West says not to look at the motives. Look at the evidence," Travis reminded his cousin. "And the evidence says that Alana and Tom have lousy alibis. Not to mention that they're behavior has been strange as hell. I thought something was weird with them."

Shane was nodding but he didn't look convinced. "I know West says to ignore the motives but I still want to know what they gain from all this."

"Let's review the usual motives then. Money?" Travis began to pace the small strip between the table and the windows. "Alana has a prenup with Martin so if she leaves him, she gets nothing. I remember Martin telling me about it before they got married. His lawyers insisted on it. But if he goes to prison for murder she gets a fortune to spend as she pleases while he rots behind bars. Remember she had access to the cufflinks. She could have planted it under Bruce's body to frame her husband."

"What does Tom get? Or do you think he's just helping Alana with an alibi? Or does he want Alana?"

Travis thought about the strange dysfunctional goings-on that day when he had talked to Caroline. Tom had been over the top protective and nothing in his demeanor spoke of a hidden passion for Alana.

"Caroline. He gets Caroline. The motive is love and money."

Deep in his gut Travis was sure he was right. That day he'd been puzzled by the behavior exhibited by Tom but now it made sense.

Tom wanted Caroline. And the money she would have too.

Alana wanted Martin's money.

"What about Iris?" Shane asked. "How does she fit into this?"

"I'm not sure," Travis admitted, his mind still whirling with all the possibilities. "Maybe she does or doesn't. I'm more worried about where Caroline fits. What if she's in on it?"

"You know what Jason would ask you. What's your gut telling you?"

Travis considered the question but his instincts had already answered it. "She's not interested. She barely glances at him when he's around. There's no way that she loves him enough to kill her husband. Hell, I don't think she even hated Bruce enough to kill him and she had ample reason to. No, my gut is telling me that Caroline is innocent."

But Alana and Tom? That was an entirely different matter.

"So what do we do now? We can't prove any of this and Prather thinks Martin is guilty. I doubt we can get him to look elsewhere by talking about gut feelings and crappy alibis."

"Let's go talk to Caroline." Travis shoved his cell in his pocket along with his key card. "Maybe she can shed some light on the relationship between Tom and Alana."

What they needed was hard proof.

Chapter Thirty-One

"Tom, what are you doing?" Caroline's voice came out as barely a whisper but he heard her anyway.

"This wasn't supposed to happen. You weren't supposed to be here and find me. Now that you have I need time to think."

Tom tapped his forehead with the gun, a frown on his boyishly handsome face.

He could take all the time in the world to think things over. In the meantime, Aubrey wasn't going to go down without a fight. She liked being on this end of a gun for the second time even less than the first. "Put the gun down, Tom. Don't do something you're going to regret for a long time after this."

Tom didn't react as she expected him to. Instead of arguing and brandishing his weapon, he threw back his head and laughed loudly, almost hysterically. "The time for regrets has already passed. I've come too far to turn back now. The only problem is that Caro shouldn't have been here. I've been trying to protect her from all this."

"Protect me from what, Tom?"

Carole had taken a tentative step closer to the gun wielding man.

Tom scowled but didn't lower his arm an inch, the muzzle still pointed directly at Caroline's heart.

"From Bruce. He wasn't good for you, Caro, but you wouldn't leave. So I got rid of him for you. But I never wanted you to know."

The blonde's mouth fell open in shock. "You killed Bruce?"

Tom took a step back to lean his hip against the sofa table. "Not personally, no."

Not personally? Then who did?

"Did you kill Iris?" Aubrey piped up, her palms sweating with fear. The only thing she knew to do was to keep him talking as long as possible until she saw a chance to get the gun. Her gaze darted around the room looking for the easiest way to escape.

Her back was to the entrance to the suite. Too far to try to outrun a man with much longer legs and arm reach. The room opened up to the sweeping patio but they were eight stories up. It was way too far to even contemplate jumping to safety, and she wasn't in the kind of shape that would allow her to climb down the balconies. No, that exit wasn't viable.

The expansive marble bathroom was behind Tom and per-haps she and Caroline could somehow sprint around him and lock themselves in, hiding behind the linen closet and the marble walls of the shower. It wasn't bulletproof but it was a better chance than they stood out here in the open with nothing between them and a gun.

It still wasn't ideal. In fact, that plan sucked because she couldn't see how they were going to get to the bathroom in the first place. Cause a diversion maybe?

But if they did, then the best play was probably to get his gun while he was distracted. It was what tipped the balance of power in his favor.

"Iris knew too much and was becoming a problem." There was a gleam in his eye that hadn't been there before, almost as if he was relishing the memory. "Alana too."

Caroline pressed a palm to her forehead. "Alana knew what was going on? Did everyone know but me?"

"Not at all." Tom waved the gun in a downward motion. "And keep your hands to your sides. No, not everyone knew. Alana wanted Martin's money and was willing to frame him for murder to get it. But she also thinks that she and I are going to ride off into the sunset together. That was not the plan."

"But you let her believe that," prodded Aubrey, trickles of sweat running down her back. "And Iris too perhaps?"

She remembered how Iris had spoken about a handsome boyfriend. Could she have been talking about Tom and not Bruce?

"I can't help what women believe."

Damn, he was one stone cold bastard and Aubrey had been up close and personal to another one – Alan Morton. But this guy didn't seem as delusional as Alan had. Tom was more calculating and methodical, eliminating threats one by one until he held all the cards.

Scary as hell to think people like this walked around looking normal.

Caroline's spine straightened even as the tension in the air grew thick. "So what now? Are you going to kill us too?"

Tom shook his head, frustration in the set of his shoulders.

"I did all this for you. For us. But now it's all ruined. You've left me with few choices."

"The police think I might have done this." Caroline's lips pressed together angrily. "You could get me thrown in prison."

Tom stepped forward, causing the two women to retreat from his stormy gaze. "That wasn't supposed to happen. That's why I'm here. To plant the murder weapon and pills in Alana's room. Then all I would have had to do is call in an anonymous tip to the cops and they would come and find it. Then Alana would be joining her husband in prison while you and I spend the money. But I guess now I'll have to hold on to her."

Aubrey and Caroline exchanged a shocked look. Tom had gone to elaborate lengths to get his hands on billions via Caroline. Killing them didn't seem to be much of an escalation.

"I'm not in love with you. I've never been in love with you. What made you think I would go off with you?"

Tom laughed again but the sound didn't sound happy. "You would have. Eventually. Once everyone you loved and depended on was gone. You would have turned to me, the only friend you had left. I would have made you happier than that asshole of a husband you had."

"That's not saying a lot," Caroline muttered, her gaze falling to the floor and then going back to Tom. "What if I keep my mouth shut? We can have the money and each other."

That's it. Make him believe there's a chance so he'll relax and put down the gun.

Tom's eyes narrowed but his smile never faltered. "My darling girl, that is not an option. I want you but if I have to choose, the money wins every single time."

"You can't have it without Caroline." At least Aubrey hoped that was the case. It would keep her friend valuable and alive, if not herself.

"Can't I? Alana is in love with me and will happily share the wealth. You see, I've thought of all the angles, little Aubrey. I'll have the money and a gorgeous woman on my arm no matter what happens."

"You've got it all planned except for one little thing," Aubrey goaded, hoping to rattle him and trying to sound brave. She didn't want him to know how truly terrified she was. "Us. We're here and I don't think you want to shoot your way out of this like it's the OK Corral. That's not a good way to keep your dirty little secret. If you run I'll give you a head start."

For all his cool bravado, Tom wasn't nearly as sure of the situation as he tried to appear. The hand that held the gun had the slightest of trembles. It might not be noticed by anyone who wasn't looking but Aubrey was scrutinizing him for the most minuscule of weaknesses. His face was sweaty and she guessed his hand was as well. The weapon might slip out of his fingers easily if he was pushed or jostled in any way.

Maybe. At this point Aubrey was grasping at hopeful straws.

"I don't think I'll need it." Tom shook his head, his cheeks a dull red either from anger or some other strong emotion that Aubrey didn't recognize. "You both have left me no choice really. You'll both have to die."

Caroline stiffened next to Aubrey and she wanted to reach out and comfort her new friend. She'd already been through hell this week and now a family friend had just announced this was their last day on earth.

The hell it was. Aubrey wasn't about to die like a dog in the streets at the hands of a thug after money. The only difference in this asshole and the guys she used to see rob the local liquor stores in Chicago was the price tag of the clothes they wore. Either way they were just punks. She sure as hell wasn't going to let this one get the best of her.

"You're going to gun us down in cold blood," Aubrey snorted, hoping Tom couldn't hear the pounding of her heartbeat that sounded like a drum in her ears. Her stomach clenched, wanting to expel the breakfast she'd consumed but she swallowed down the acidic bile that had gathered in the back of her throat. "I'll be shocked if the cops don't have you in custody within an hour. You're dreaming if you think you'll get away with this."

"I'm not planning to take the fall for this but even if I was caught it wouldn't matter. Money talks. There are two kinds of justice systems – one for the rich and one for everyone else."

"There's just one problem with that," Caroline smirked. "You're not rich. Bruce said you're broke as hell, in fact. You're one of the little people, Tom. How does it feel? And don't say Alana will bail you out. With all those billions she can move on to someone even younger and better looking than you are. But you do have the right coloring…for orange."

Tom stepped forward and lifted his arm, holding the gun straight at Caroline. His lips were twisted into an evil sort of snarl that changed his features from handsome to sinister in a mere second.

"Holding this gun I don't feel so little. But they won't come after me. Not when this is a murder-suicide. You shot Aubrey because she was on to you about killing Bruce. Then you turned the gun on yourself. Not bad, actually. I'll place the knife in your pocket and no one will question it."

The gun swung to Aubrey and her knees began to shake even as her heart plummeted to her stomach. She wasn't sure how she was even standing on her own two feet at the moment, but terror had frozen her in place. She blinked as tears began to well up in her eyes. Caroline's hand grasped her own, tightening into a painful grip that kept Aubrey from screaming at the top of her lungs. She wouldn't give this bastard the satisfaction.

"Are you ready to die, Aubrey?"

Chapter Thirty-Two

"DID YOU EVER find your girl?"

Lotte, the housekeeper they'd spoken to about Caroline was in the corridor when Travis and Shane exited the elevator. Shane immediately smiled at the older woman who was cleaning a room a few doors down from Martin's suite.

"Kind of," Shane chuckled. "What are you doing on this floor? I thought you worked on ten."

Humming a soft tune, Lotte emptied a waste basket into a trash bag. "I usually do ten and eleven but we've got a girl out sick today which means the rest of us have to pick up a little extra. Now tell me, how can you *kind of* find a person? Did she turn you down?"

Shane grinned and scratched his chin. "Let's go with that. How are you, Lotte?"

"I'm fine," she drawled with a laugh. "My day is almost over so I can't complain. How are you gentlemen?"

Coughing, probably at being called a gentleman, Shane pointed to Martin's door. "We're good. Just going to visit a friend on this floor."

"Enjoy yourselves. I'm going–"

Lotte didn't get any farther. The sound of two gunshots, one after the other, rang out, jerking Travis out of his reverie and into fight or flight mode. Both he and Shane pushed Lotte to the floor, their bodies covering hers before looking up cautiously. Adrenaline coursed through Travis's veins and his muscles tensed as shouts could be heard coming from Martin's suite.

Ignoring the sputtering of his heart Travis sprung to his feet, ripping the pass key out of the door lock from the room Lotte had been cleaning. He didn't bother to look behind him knowing that Shane would be right on his heels.

"Call 911," Travis yelled over his shoulder as he hurriedly tried to shove the card into the slot. His shaking fingers made it difficult and a string of curses fell from his lips even as blood roared in his ears.

Get to Aubrey. Get to her. Protect her.

He didn't want to think about what was behind this door or what could have happened. Unarmed and completely in the dark, he was in no state to be able to deal with any threat to the woman he loved. All he had was himself and his determination. Hopefully it would be enough.

Crouching close to the floor, he slowly pushed open the door, peering cautiously around it. Travis didn't see anyone and swung the door wider, Shane right behind him. They stayed low to the ground, not wanting to become the target of a shooter that may or may not be in this hotel room. Travis prayed that neither of them were here and that they were still downstairs in the spa or at the bar.

Please don't let my girl be hurt.

"Help. Please help us."

The bloody scene he came upon punched him in the gut and almost had him doubled over in exquisite pain.

Both women were on the floor, Aubrey on her back in a pool of blood while Caroline, also covered in crimson knelt next to her friend, one hand pressed to Aubrey's abdomen, the other bloody and mangled, hung uselessly at her side.

"Caroline? Aubrey?" Travis knelt next to the woman he loved, his breaking heart pounding painfully against his ribs and thick acid choking off his oxygen. Tears sprang to his eyes as his gaze ran up and down Aubrey, so still and ghostly white. "Aubrey, baby, can you hear me?"

"It was Tom." Caroline coughed, barely able to speak, not looking much better than Aubrey. "We found him trying to plant evidence against Alana and so he tried to shoot us. Make it look like a murder-suicide. We rushed him to get the gun but we were both hit."

Shane's hand squeezed Travis's shoulder but he barely felt it, numbness beginning to seep into every crevice of his being. If he lost Aubrey...

Don't. Don't even fucking think it.

"Keep pressure on that gunshot," Shane ordered. "You're doing a great job. Lotte called 911 and there is an ambulance on the way. Where is Tom?"

Caroline glanced over to the French doors that led to the patio that were wide open. "He went out there and climbed down, I think. We managed to get the gun from him and he ran."

"Good job," Travis praised, his voice cracking as his hands settled on Aubrey's blood soaked belly. "You're exhausted—let me take over. Just slide your hand away and I'll move mine to take their place."

"I'm going after Lovell," Shane announced, levering to his feet. "Will you be okay?"

"Go. I can't leave her."

I'll never leave you, baby. Don't leave me. Please don't leave me. I love you. So damn much.

Caroline was shaking her head, tears streaming down her face and Travis realized he too was crying, his vision blurred. His entire body trembled with the very real fear that he just might lose this woman just as he had found her.

"Let me take over, Caro," Travis said quietly, the words coming out like a shovel scraped against a gravel road. "You're going to pass out."

The young woman didn't budge. "I'm...okay."

He slid his hands until they lay on top of hers while keeping his eye on Aubrey. If anything she was paler than she was before which Travis didn't think was even possible, but now her lips had disappeared into her face and purple shadows bruised the flesh under her eyes, her skin almost translucent. He could barely catch his breath as she slipped further from him with each passing second.

This is all my fault. If I'd figured it out sooner this wouldn't have happened.

"It's okay," Travis cajoled, ignoring the pain in his chest and gut, the utter failure that had allowed this to happen. "I've got her. It's okay."

Caroline's fingers slid out from under his as her eyes rolled back in her head, slumping on the floor next to Aubrey. A flurry of footsteps entered the suite and then the EMTs were there, asking questions and pushing him aside.

He watched them work, silent on the outside but begging for a miracle inside. Things he'd never say. Things they'd never do. So many "if onlys" but the one that wouldn't leave him alone was that he should have known. He should have been here sooner. He should have known Tom would do this.

Travis had failed to protect her and he would never forgive himself.

Even if Aubrey managed to survive he couldn't expect – couldn't begin to ask – for absolution. This was a sin he'd carry with him forever.

"Sir? Sir, do you want to ride with them?"

"What?" Travis shook his head trying to clear his vision, fogged with tears. It had been years since he had cried, nothing touching him enough, but he doubted these would be the last today. "Yes. Yes, I want to ride with them."

If she lets me I'll never leave her.

"Follow us then."

IVs and tubes were now attached to both women as they lay on the gurneys, the men wheeling them out of the room and down the hall as quickly as possible.

"How is Caroline? I think she's in shock."

He already knew Aubrey was in serious condition simply by observing the expressions on the EMT's face.

"The blonde? She's got a gunshot wound to the hand but I think she'll be okay. It's the brunette that we're worried about. They're prepping the OR. She's going straight into surgery once she's stable enough."

Travis didn't have to be told. It was her only chance.

If Shane didn't catch Tom, Travis would.

The man would wish he'd never been born.

This was Travis's solemn vow.

✦   ✦   ✦

THE SMELL OF antiseptic and blood stung Travis's nostrils as he paced up and down the emergency waiting room. Aubrey had been in one of the exam rooms for what seemed like hours as they tried to stabilize her before taking her back to surgery. He scraped his fingers through his hair once again as his stomach twisted into knots.

His sweet Aubrey might not make it.

She'd taken a bullet to her abdomen and lost copious amounts of blood. Travis truly didn't know how anyone could survive something like that but he couldn't even wrap his mind around the thought he might actually lose her.

She was so alive. So vibrant and beautiful.

They'd spoken words of love and talked about the future but now all of that was in jeopardy.

"Here's some coffee. You look like you could use it. It's probably terrible but I think we're in for a long night."

Shane held two paper cups of steaming liquid and Travis took one gratefully. Sipping at the bitter brew, he grimaced before falling back into one of the chairs that felt like it had been designed by the Marque de Sade. Much longer out here and he'd be ready for one of the patient rooms himself.

"Did you talk to Prather?"

Shane had chased Tom but the man had jumped into an arriving vehicle in the valet parking circle, accelerating out of the parking lot. By the time Shane had procured a car to chase the fugitive Tom was long gone.

Or hiding somewhere in a back alley or side street.

At this point it didn't matter. The only important thing was Aubrey and her survival. Travis would find Tom Lovell although it would have to wait for another day.

"I did. I gave him my statement and now he's back there with Caroline. The doctor told him to make it fast because the pain drip they gave her is going to kick in and she'll fall asleep."

Mercifully. The bullet had practically taken off two fingers but a specialist had been called in and they were planning to do surgery first thing in the morning.

"Is he letting Martin go?" There was a part of Travis that still believed that Prather wasn't going to let go of his original theory. "Does he have men looking for Lovell?"

"He does. I heard him on the phone alerting the airlines and bus stations too. If Tom is smart he already dumped the car he stole. Lucky for us he wasn't prepared for this. He ran out empty-handed. No cash. No identification. Nothing. As for Martin, a judge has to let him go but his attorney has that in the works. It shouldn't be long now."

"That only makes Lovell more dangerous. Fuck, how did I not know, Shane? It seems so clear now. If I'd known earlier–"

"Fucking stop it," Shane commanded, sitting next to Travis. "Just stop this shit. Hell, the cops didn't even know so how were you supposed to? You figured it out. Martin's getting out of jail and the police are looking for Lovell."

"I was too late."

Shane put his hand on Travis's shoulder in a comforting gesture that wasn't unappreciated, but it didn't help the ever growing lump of dread that had taken up residence in his stomach. To be honest, he wasn't sure he was even going to be able to keep down this horrific coffee.

"Aubrey's going to make it," Shane stated, certainty in his tone. "You forget that it wasn't all that long ago that I was lying in a hospital bed with a bullet in my gut. Now here I am dancing around and basically making trouble. I was okay and she's going to be okay too. Believe it. She has a lot to live for."

Acid churned in Travis's stomach and he tossed the half drank cup in a trash can without a backward glance. Food and drink were strictly off limits if he didn't want to disgrace himself by hanging his head in the nearest toilet bowl.

"What if she isn't?" Travis asked quietly as if he was trying to keep the secret from himself. If he didn't say it too loudly he might not hear the words and then it couldn't possibly happen. "What if she doesn't make it?"

Shane grabbed Travis by his shirt and dragged him to his feet so they were nose to nose. "Don't even say that. You two are going to live happily fucking ever after, you got that? Someone has to. It sure as shit won't ever be me. She's going to pull through and you're going to have six kids all named Shane, you asshole."

Travis knew that Shane had some deep personal crap that he kept well hidden. There was a woman, but who she was and what she meant was a mystery.

"I'm not naming my kids Shane."

Both men began to smile and then the tears started. Travis

let them fall unashamedly and Shane wasn't too much of a man to join in.

"Sure you are. It's a great name. Boy or girl."

If Aubrey made it through this Travis would name their kids after the doctors that saved her life.

In fact, he didn't need kids, or a house, or a dog, or any of that stuff to be happy.

He just needed Aubrey.

Chapter Thirty-Three

EVERY BONE AND muscle in Aubrey's body ached. She tried to move her arms and legs but they felt weighted down, heavy like lead. Panicking, her lids flew open and she groaned as bright sunlight bore into her corneas, sending shards of pain through her skull.

"Easy, baby. Easy. Everything's okay. You're fine."

Those smooth, hushed tones belonged to Travis and she felt herself relaxing under his warm touch, his hands running up and down her arm while his fingers brushed at her cheek.

"Travis," she croaked, her throat parched and sore. "Where? What?"

"Let's set you up a little and get you something to drink. Then we can talk. You've had everybody mighty worried."

Travis pressed a button on the side of the bed and the mattress lifted her up until she could finally look into his warm green eyes. He poured some water from a plastic pitcher into a glass and held the straw up to her lips to let her drink greedily.

"Not too much until the doctor takes a look at you. I don't want you to be sick."

She swallowed the cool liquid that tasted like the sweetest

ambrosia. A sweeping gaze around the room told her she was in the hospital but her mind didn't seem to want to work out how or why.

"I feel like a truck hit me."

Travis grinned and chuckled, pressing a chaste kiss to her forehead before going over to the windows and shutting the blinds. The relief to her pounding skull was immediate and welcome.

"I'm not surprised, considering everything you've been through."

"You look awful. Have you been sick too?"

Now that she could really look at Travis, she was shocked. He looked like he was dead and didn't have enough sense to lie down. His skin was pasty, his eyes bloodshot and red-rimmed, and his clothes were hanging off his body as if he hadn't eaten in days.

"I've had better weeks, baby. But seeing you with your eyes open makes up for everything. Do you remember why you're here?"

She was about to shake her head and say no, but then flashes of memory ran through her head and she remembered that afternoon and Tom Lovell.

"Tom shot me." Tears began to well up and then another memory had her struggling to sit up. "Caroline! Is Caroline okay? Oh God, he said he was going to make it look like a murder-suicide."

Travis gently pressed her back to the bed, whispering soothing words as he stroked her damp forehead. "Caro's fine. She left the hospital yesterday after surgery on her hand. You were the one that took the brunt of things. You were the one we were all worried about."

Gulping in air, Aubrey let her heart rate return to something close to normal, although with all the tubes and machines hooked up to her she wasn't sure what normal was anymore.

"We rushed him. We knew we only had one chance to get the gun from him."

From the pained expression on Travis's face he already knew the story from Caroline.

"You were very brave, baby. I only wish I'd been there to protect you. I'm so sorry I wasn't there when you needed me."

She lifted her left hand, unencumbered by an IV, and cupped his handsome face. Several days' growth of whiskers brushed her palm but she welcomed the roughness against her fingers.

"It wasn't your fault. We caught Tom trying to plant evidence against Alana. If you had been there he would have tried to kill you too."

A muscle jerked in Travis's jaw and she heard him take a few deep breaths. "If I'd been there you wouldn't have been in front of that gun. I would have taken that bullet. That's what a man is supposed to do."

The Anderson men had a code of conduct that didn't leave much room for error. Travis wasn't cutting himself any slack even though he had worked hard to clear her and his friend's names.

"Let's hope it doesn't come to that. I'm kind of hoping actually that I'm done being in dangerous situations where you have to drag me to the hospital. How about we become the world's most boring couple?"

Travis's eyes closed for a long moment and when he opened them she could see them bright with unshed tears, but he smiled and looked at her as if she was the most precious thing he'd ever seen.

"That sounds like a damn good idea. I think you and I should retire from sleuthing."

"That is an excellent idea."

The booming voice came from behind Travis and he moved aside to reveal West Anderson and Aubrey's sister Gigi. Gigi squealed, racing forward to hug Aubrey but somehow managing to be gentle with her sister's tired and sore body.

"Leave them alone, West. They were just trying to help out a friend." Gigi leaned down and kissed Aubrey's cheek. "You scared me out of my wits, sis! You've been asleep for days."

Aubrey frowned and clutched her sister's hand tightly. "Just how long have I been out?"

"Four days," Gigi replied, cradling Aubrey's hand next to her cheek as she started to cry. "So many times we didn't think you were going to pull through. Travis hasn't left your side since it happened."

Aubrey gave a warm smile to the blushing man standing next to her bed. That explained why he looked like a walking zombie. Someone had obviously brought him clean clothes but she'd bet a wad of cash he wasn't eating or sleeping well, if at all.

"When did you get here?"

West leaned against the wall of the room watching his fiancée indulgently. "We took the jet as soon as Shane called us. Jason and Brinley are here too and they went down to get something to eat but they'll be back in a few minutes. I hate to break up this party and all but has anyone told the doctor you're awake? They might be interested in this development."

Travis pressed the call button. "Consider them notified."

Within a few minutes the nurses and doctor were bustling in and out. Everyone was shooed out of the room while Aubrey was being examined and the doctor seemed pleased with her progress.

"You scared your family, young lady," the older man scolded but she could tell he was teasing because of his kind smile. "We repaired the internal bleeding but we had to take out your spleen. If everything keeps improving like this you can go home in a few days."

That sounded like heaven even if "home" was a hotel room with room service. She thanked the doctor, truly grateful she'd been given a second chance. She and Travis had so much more living to do. So many plans and dreams and she intended to live them all.

Travis joined her, propping himself on the edge of the bed. He'd sent everyone back to the hotel, but Gigi was coming back tonight to sit with Aubrey so that Travis could finally get some sleep. Aubrey had insisted on it and he seemed too exhausted to argue.

"Tell me what's gone on while I've been asleep. Is Martin out of jail? What happened to Alana and Tom?"

Travis scraped his hand down his face and sighed deeply before answering. She had a feeling she wasn't going to like what he had to say.

"Martin is out of jail but Alana has been arrested for accessory to murder, which isn't a shock. Tom is on the run but I've got a private investigator out looking for him in addition to all the resources of Detective Prather's office. He doesn't have the resources to look outside of Florida."

"You hired someone?"

It didn't sound like the hands-on Travis she knew so well, but then his hands had been full with her these last several days.

"I did. An old military buddy of West's named Wyatt Stone. He helped West get Gigi to safety when they were on the run. West said the guy can handle himself and knows a thing or two about covert operations. He seemed like the right man for the job. Jason has been trying to recruit him."

Aubrey digested the information but it didn't assuage the hunger to find out more about the time she'd been unconscious. "Do you think you'll find him?"

Travis leaned down, their gazes locked. She'd never seen him look that intense before, not even when he'd told her he loved her. "Absolutely, and that's a promise. I will find Tom and I will bring him to justice for what he did."

"He did it for the money. At least that's what he told us. He wanted Caroline too, but she wanted nothing to do with him so he said he'd make do with Alana."

"Ah yes, Alana. She wanted the money as well but couldn't get it because of her prenup. So she conspired with Tom to frame Martin for Bruce's murder. She was having an affair with Tom and she wanted him and the life of luxury."

It was still hard for Aubrey to wrap her mind around. "So they killed Bruce because of the insider trading?"

Travis chuckled and shook his head. "That's not why. With

urging from Tom, Iris encouraged Bruce in the insider trading. She was his mistress but she was also sleeping with Tom. Both women believed Tom loved them. But Tom wanted Bruce out of the way so he could have Caroline."

"Wait. Iris was sleeping with Tom? Did he kill her too?"

The twists and turns were almost too much for her brain, already addled with painkillers. She had to listen and concentrate carefully to be able to decipher Travis's words.

"Tom did kill Iris. He put some of Alana's Ambien in Iris's champagne and she fell asleep. He carried her out to the pool, dropped her in, and she drowned."

"And he killed Bruce too? Plus tried to kill Caroline and me?"

So much violence and death for something as shallow as money. Even if it was billions.

"According to Alana, Iris killed Bruce at Tom's behest and she did it to help Tom get revenge for Bruce's shady business dealings. At least that's what she thought she was doing. Once again they used the Ambien and they slipped it in Bruce's drink. He was woozy when he went out to the tennis courts, but of course Iris could get close to him without suspicion. She stuck the knife in Bruce's heart and left him to die, tucking the cufflink underneath him to frame Martin."

Rubbing her aching temple, it all seemed so surreal, like something out of a movie.

"What's going to happen to Alana?"

Aubrey had never felt comfortable around the woman and now she knew why. But she still did feel sorry for her. She'd been taken in by a handsome sociopath.

"She's going to do some serious time, but she's already made a deal with the DA to spill everything she knows for a lighter sentence. Martin has begun divorce proceedings, of course. Once he found out he was the patsy in all this he wasn't a happy man. The whole insider trading thing was just a ruse so that Martin would have a motive for killing Bruce. The fact that you got caught up in all this was just bad luck and timing."

"The story of my life," she murmured, thinking how close she came to being arrested for a crime she didn't commit. "Thank you for never giving up and not caring about...well...you know."

Although after all she'd been through the past didn't look nearly as bad. She'd made some bad choices but she'd been young. She'd learned and moved on, and wasn't that the important point from all this? Sleeping around didn't make her a tramp or a floozy but she'd allowed other people to make her feel that way. She didn't have to answer to anyone about what she'd done. It was none of their business.

"I don't want you to give it a second thought." Travis's words were filled with urgency and love. She could feel it as if it were a warm blanket wrapping around her by a roaring fireplace after a long walk through the snow. It felt comfortable and safe but there was passion as well. "I love you. And when I thought I was going to lose you..."

His voice broke off and a few tears escaped to slide down his cheeks. She pulled his head down to hers and pressed her lips against his and was shocked to feel this big, strong man trembling in her arms.

"I'm okay. It's all right."

"It's not okay. That bullet should have hit me. I love you so damn much and I can't imagine this world without you. I kept praying and hoping. Shane told me I had to believe. I want you forever. The thought of losing you was more painful than anything I could imagine. Please say you love me and that you'll let me worship and adore you for the rest of my life."

His voice was hoarse but the love behind it was clear. She'd never been this loved before, and despite the aches and pains still present in her body happiness fizzed in her veins like bubbly champagne. Everything was going to be fine.

"Well…" Aubrey pretended to think about it but she couldn't suppress a smile of pure joy. "I guess I could let you. I mean, I don't have any other plans or anything. But there is one thing though."

Travis's lips ghosted over her own – once, twice, three times, making her shiver with pleasure.

"Anything. You name it."

Aubrey let her fingers slide through his thick dark hair and gazed into the face of her future. "You have to let me love and adore you right back. That's the only way I'll agree."

"Deal."

There'd been too many tears. It was time to look to the future. Not even Travis could make everything perfect and happy every single day but there would always be love, and that's all that really mattered anyway.

Chapter Thirty-Four

TRAVIS AND WYATT Stone climbed up the wrought iron stairs to the second floor of the stucco apartment building. In a quiet suburb outside of Newark, New Jersey the town was the perfect place to raise a family with its tree lined streets and friendly atmosphere. The apartment complex was located near an elementary school and a large mall that was currently bustling with shoppers.

In fact, it was that very mall that had given them their first lead in over a month.

The local police had already raided the home, an end unit that overlooked a park with a running path and playground. Travis and Wyatt had promised to hang back until they received the all clear, but they'd made it plain that they wouldn't be left out altogether. Wyatt and Travis had done the heavy lifting in this investigation, after all. Travis simply wanted Lovell to know that he would always be there.

At the trial.

At the sentencing.

At any parole hearings in the future.

Travis would be there to make sure the authorities were

aware of all the facts. Tom Lovell had killed two people and tried to kill two more. And that's what they knew about. He could have other victims strewn across the United States that no one was aware of.

Prather and the local lead detective exited the apartment and gave Travis and Wyatt a nod. "We've got him. You were right. He was shacked up here with another girlfriend. That guy sure has a way with the ladies."

When Travis had seen how smoothly Lovell had played both Alana and Iris, he'd postulated that there might be more women out there. Women who might be dazzled enough to give Tom refuge while he was on the run. It was there that Wyatt had started his investigation, and with some questioning of Tom's friends and neighbors he'd found the identity of a third woman. Surveillance on that female had proven fruitless until she'd stopped into a local retailer and purchased a supply of men's clothing, all in Lovell's size.

Armed with that proof, Stone had used his limitless patience to sit outside the apartment building for weeks watching nothing but the comings and goings of the girlfriend. But Wyatt had known that with each passing day Tom would feel a little bit safer and eventually cabin fever and inactivity would force him out of the house. Then they'd know for sure. It had taken weeks but Wyatt had spotted Lovell this morning going on a Starbucks run.

It had taken several hours to gather the personnel and put together a plan, but the SWAT team had just delivered the arrest warrant from Florida. Tom would be heading back to face trial for his actions.

"When will you send him back?" Travis asked as he waited for a glimpse of the man who had been his soul focus for the last month and a half.

"In the morning," Prather replied, still not acting very friendly despite being handed a double murderer on a platter. He had egg on his face regarding Martin's arrest so Travis didn't expect that any of them were in the detective's good graces. "He'll spend the night in county and then me and my men will escort him back. The DA is already prepping the case for trial but I'm sure he'll offer some kind of deal. Who knows? Maybe he'll confess and save the taxpayers some money. Seems like the type that might want to brag about it."

Two uniformed cops escorted the woman out, her hands cuffed behind her back, tears running down her face. Travis felt a twinge of sympathy as she'd been taken in like so many others, but giving aid and comfort to a known criminal was never a good idea no matter how charming and loving he seemed.

Standing in the middle of the walkway Travis waited, his hands curled into fists, nails digging into the meat of his palms. He just needed this one moment and then he could go home. Back to his friends, family, career, and of course Aubrey. She was finally feeling more like herself although she still sometimes had nightmares about that day. She worked with a therapist but the doctor had been brutally honest with both Aubrey and Caroline. They might always have flashbacks to that moment, although they should get fewer and far between. Being shot at was a life-changing moment and the brain was a tricky thing. It wasn't going to let go of the trauma all that easily.

Two more uniformed officers finally exited the apartment, this time with Lovell between them. The man looked a little roughed up, a bruise beginning to form on his cheekbone, as if he'd resisted attempts to bring him in but otherwise it was the same smirking Tom Lovell.

They'd all been fooled.

Lovell was cuffed and each arm was held by a cop as they escorted him right to Travis, stopping about three feet away. Travis studied the man that had shot Aubrey in cold blood, leaving her for dead.

"Hello, Tom."

Lovell smiled but it looked more like a snarl. "Hello, Travis. Funny meeting you here."

"It's not funny at all. I've been looking for you, actually. You hurt something of mine. You shouldn't have done that."

If Lovell was afraid he didn't show it outwardly but Travis did see the man's chest rising and falling slightly faster than before. It could have been for a myriad of reasons, not just Travis. Lovell was losing his freedom as of this moment so that might account for the agitation.

"I'm not sure what you're talking about. This is all a misunderstanding."

The corner of Travis's mouth quirked up. Lovell was going to go down with the ship. He'd never confess because he believed he could talk and charm his way out of anything.

"Aubrey and Caroline are alive, Tom. Alive. They have an interesting story to tell. Alana's singing like a bird, too."

There it was. Lovell's smile faltered but for mere seconds. Travis was sure he was already formulating his next sure fire, foolproof plan.

"I'm sure I don't know what you mean, Travis. This has all been a huge mistake. You'll see."

Travis leaned forward but the cops stepped back, feeling the rage that was carefully held in check.

"You made a huge mistake, Lovell. You hurt people I care about. I'm going to make it my personal mission to see you rot behind bars. I'll clear my desk of any and all projects and make it my life's work. Do you get what I'm saying? I'm going to become the thing that makes you wake up in the middle of the night screaming and covered with sweat."

With that, Travis turned on his heel, not bothering to see Tom's reaction. It didn't matter because Travis had spoken the truth. He would make sure Tom faced justice for what he'd done. Legally, of course. He was no vigilante. But he wanted to ensure that Lovell knew that there was someone out there that gave a shit.

Travis and Wyatt climbed into the rental car and backed out of the parking lot, pulling into the traffic headed to the airport. It was time to go home.

"So did you get what you came for, boss?" Wyatt asked softly, his expression neutral but Travis had learned a few things about the man in the last few days. Wyatt Stone might not show much emotion but there was a hell of a lot going on underneath that serene exterior. Things Stone didn't talk about and probably never would.

"I did. I wanted him to know that I wouldn't give up, no matter what. Not sure it made any difference though. I doubt he really thinks he's going to be tried and convicted."

Wyatt shrugged, never taking his eyes from the road. "I've known men like that. They live in a different world from you and I. They're free from consequences there and they're more than a little narcissistic. But I think you've got him dead to rights this time. Unless there are some weird technicalities, he's going to prison."

It would never be enough but Wyatt was right. Lovell would never change. Put him behind bars and move on with life.

Travis had kept his promise to Aubrey.

✦   ✦   ✦

"You're home."

Aubrey had been curled up on the couch watching television when she'd heard Travis's truck pull up in front of the house. Now she was wrapped in his arms and the last two lonely days were erased from her memory, joy curling her toes and making every cell in her body alive and tingling.

"I am home. You shouldn't have waited up. You need your rest."

Sighing, she pressed another kiss to his hard jaw line, a light stubble tickling her lips. "I've been resting for weeks. I'm ready to get back to living life again. I'm not made to watch television and eat chocolates all day."

While recovering, Travis had spoiled her terribly and it was time she did some spoiling of her own. She knew very well where he'd been the last few days. He hadn't hidden anything from her as he'd methodically hunted down Tom Lovell. He'd been calm and sweet since the shooting but she'd been aware of the anger simmering just under the surface. Travis was a protective man and someone had hurt people he cared about. He wasn't going to just sit back and observe. He was a man of action.

"As soon as the doctor says you can go back to work and not a day sooner. Try and enjoy your time off while I'm being tortured by your temp replacement. I think she hates me."

"More like she's terrified of you," Aubrey retorted. "You're constantly barking at her about something."

"Because she's constantly screwing something up," Travis countered. "Not everyone is as efficient as you are."

If the man she loved wanted to give her a compliment she wasn't going to argue. Instead she took a deep breath and asked the question that had been hanging between them since he walked in the door.

"So you found him. Did you talk to him?"

"I did and he didn't say anything that I didn't expect him to." Travis nodded and pulled her closer. Aubrey leaned into his body, drawing strength and warmth from his nearness. "There was no grand confession. He'll deny to his last breath. Right now he's in custody and headed back to Florida where he'll face trial along with Alana."

Not sure what to say, Aubrey simply chose to say nothing at all. She was glad Tom Lovell was behind bars. Sometimes she felt like he was behind every bush and tree, watching and waiting to try and kill her again. His incarceration would help with the fear and nightmares but nothing was going to erase the memories.

She'd grown incredibly close to Caroline in the past month and a half as they'd both healed from their wounds. Caroline had moved to Montana, wanting nothing to do with her old life in New York City. Travis had given her a job heading up social media for Anderson Industries and so far she seemed to be doing a great job.

"Good. I want to start thinking about the future and not dwell on the past."

"I'm so glad you feel that way, baby. I have just the thing to help you with that."

"How do you–"

She didn't get to finish her question. Travis had gracefully fallen to one knee, her hands still clasped in his own. Faced with the sight of him before her, somehow she managed to stay upright and conscious. Barely.

"Aubrey, I love you more every day. Like you, I want to think about the future. You are it. My home. My heart. My world. Will you make me the happiest man in Montana and do me the honor of becoming my wife?"

Like all the too handsome Anderson men, Travis was beaming and showing off that sexy dimple in his cheek. He was pretty sure of her answer but he didn't appear overly confident.

Just in love.

"Yes," she whispered, a catch in her tight throat. "A million times yes."

A small velvet box appeared from his pocket and then a gorgeous platinum ring with three emerald cut diamonds was slid on her finger. He stood and pulled her in for another kiss. Then another. And then another. By the time he stood back to survey her hot cheeks and dreamy eyes he was grinning from ear to ear.

"I think it's time to start our new life, Mrs. Anderson. Any objections?"

She couldn't think of one.

She had everything she'd ever dreamed of.

Thank you for reading Danger Incorporated – Indecent Danger

Sign up to be notified of Olivia's new releases:

Newsletter Sign Up

http://eepurl.com/Y6aof

About The Author

Olivia Jaymes is a wife, mother, lover of sexy romance, and caffeine addict. She lives with her husband and son in central Florida and spends her days with handsome alpha males and spunky heroines.

She is currently working on a series of full-length novels called The Cowboy Justice Association. It's a contemporary romance series about lawmen in southern Montana who work to keep the peace but can't seem to find it in their own lives in addition to the erotic romance novella series – Military Moguls and the romantic suspense series – Danger Incorporated.

Visit Olivia Jaymes at

www.OliviaJaymes.com

Danger Incorporated

Damsel In Danger

Hiding From Danger

Discarded Heart Novella (US Kindle Only)

Cowboy Justice Association

Cowboy Command

Justice Healed

Cowboy Truth

Cowboy Famous

Cowboy Cool

Imperfect Justice

The Deputies

Military Moguls

Champagne and Bullets

Diamonds and Revolvers

Caviar and Covert Ops

Emeralds, Rubies, and Camouflage

www.ingramcontent.com/pod-product-compliance
Lightning Source LLC
Chambersburg PA
CBHW020308200626
46814CB00006BA/2142